SWEET TEA SUNRISE

RACHEL HANNA

CHAPTER 1

*M*ia stared at the computer screen with Kate and Evie standing over her like that one teacher she hated in high school. Of course, he'd had every reason to look over her shoulder since she'd cheated off the nerdy girl beside her for the entire semester.

"Well, what does it say?" Kate asked.

The whole day had been a blur after they'd managed to pull off a secret celebrity wedding for Lana Blaze. It had definitely been one of the highlights of Mia's life to be able to hug Lana's neck and take photos at her flashy wedding. She'd never forget the feeling as she watched the motorcade pull away, a big check in her hand, knowing she'd accomplished something big with her new sister.

Now, she was looking at her laptop screen, her eyes wide as saucers. The DNA site said there was another match, and she was afraid to click any further.

"I can't seem to make my finger move," Mia said,

her voice shaking. The last thing she expected was another match. What if it was another sister? Or a brother? She'd always wanted one of each.

"Come on, Aunt Mia!" Evie prodded. She had all the patience of a wild fox on speed.

"Do you want me to do it?" Cooper asked. She looked up at him and shook her head.

"No, but thanks. I just need to take a breath." Why was this so hard for her? Kate had brought wonderful things to her life, so a new family member would do the same, right? Or maybe it would shake up the delicate balance they had right now.

She took a few deep breaths and then looked back at the screen. Without giving herself time to overthink it, she clicked on the link. Blinking her eyes a few times as if she was seeing things that weren't there, she stared at the words.

"Does that say…"

"A father connection," Kate said, finishing her sentence, the words coming out of her mouth slowly.

Mia couldn't believe it. That had to be wrong. Her father? There had to be some mistake.

"Wow, Aunt Mia! Isn't this great news? Your father!" Evie hugged her from behind. "I'm so excited for you."

Mia said nothing, but stood up and walked to the kitchen, pouring herself a glass of water. She gripped the edge of the countertop with one hand and downed the glass of water with the other.

"Are you okay?" Kate asked, touching Mia's shoulder.

"I don't know," Mia said, softly.

So many times in her life, she'd dreamed of what having a father would be like. There were certain dreams she had in her head, little scenes that would play out in her lowest moments, in those times she really needed a dad.

Taking her to the father daughter dance at school.

Teaching her how to fly a kite.

Tearing up when she put on her prom dress.

Telling silly dad jokes at the dinner table.

Walking her down the aisle at her imaginary wedding.

She could see him vividly in her mind, but never did she really think he existed. He was more of a figment of her imagination, a mixture of all the good things about fathers.

The man, no matter who he was, would never live up to her dreams about him. She'd had years to conjure him up, many times feeling angry at her mother for never talking about him. She just assumed he was a bad guy in reality since her mother refused to talk about him. But at least her brain would allow him to be the best dad ever to walk the Earth.

"Are you going to send him a message?" Evie asked, excitement in her voice.

"I don't know," Mia said again. She didn't know anything right now.

"Say, Evie, do you want to walk down to the lake with me? I'm scouting some fishing spots," Cooper suddenly said.

"I don't fish," Evie said, laughing.

"Well, come help me find a spot anyway," he said.

Mia knew he was trying to help by taking Evie out

of the house. She loved her niece, but Evie was persistent and often didn't recognize other people's emotions.

"Come sit down," Kate said, pulling on her arm. Mia put the glass of water back on the counter and followed her sister.

She slowly sat down in the fluffy arm chair next to the fireplace and sighed. "I never expected this."

"But, it's good news, right? I mean, it looks like you're going to find your father."

Mia looked at her. "What if he doesn't want to know me?"

"He obviously put his DNA into the database, Mia. Surely it's because he wants to find you."

Mia stood up and walked over to the mantle. It had always been one of her favorite parts of the house with its carved wood, taken from an old tree on the property so many decades ago. It also held one of her favorite photos of her and her mother in a white, wrought iron frame.

She picked it up and ran her index finger across her mother's striking cheekbones, the same ones she saw when she looked at Evie. "You know, she was a fantastic mother. She tried so hard to make sure I never wanted for anything. I know she wanted to stand in for my missing father, but I don't know if it's because he didn't want me or maybe he never knew about me."

"What if he didn't know about you *and* he wants to know you? That's a possibility too, you know."

Mia nodded before putting the photo back on the

mantle. "I guess so. I just don't know how much more I can take."

"What do you mean?"

She sat back down and leaned her head back. "Losing my Momma was the worst thing that's ever happened to me. But, finding you and Evie has been the best."

"Aw. Thanks."

Mia looked at her. "As much as I love you both, I don't know that I can take more upheaval in my life right now. I feel so emotional these days, and I couldn't take my father pushing me away right now. It would just be too much loss, I think."

Kate leaned forward and touched her knee. "I get it. Trust me."

"I'm sorry, Kate. I know hearing me complain must be hard for you. You didn't get to know Momma, and your adoptive father sounds like a piece of work. I have no room to whine."

Kate smiled. "That's what sisters are for, right? To whine and complain? Or is it *drink* wine and complain?"

"I think it's the second one," Mia said with a laugh.

"Look, I wasn't going to tell you this, but I deactivated my DNA site account."

"What? Why?"

"Because I can only handle so much too. I'm glad we found each other, but I don't need anyone else. I was afraid long lost cousins would start appearing, and I'd be going all over the country trying to reconnect with all of these people."

"What about your father? Maybe he'll find you too."

Kate shook her head. "Sometimes I think it's better to let sleeping dogs lie. I already have one louse of a father. I don't need another one."

"Are you sure you want to give up?"

"I'm sure that I want to focus on my new sister and my daughter for awhile. Maybe one day I'll reactivate my account and look for my birth father, but things are good right now. Why rock the boat?"

Mia chuckled under her breath. "My boat's about to get rocked whether I like it or not."

"You could always deactivate your account too."

Mia shook her head. "Nah. I'm way too curious for that. I have to know one way or another."

She stood up and walked back to her computer. As she looked at the flashing cursor, she poised her fingers over the keys and began typing.

My name is Mia Carter, and I live in Georgia. I realize this might come as a shock to you, but it appears that you're my father. If you'd like to chat, please send me a message.

Before she could talk herself out of it, she clicked send and shut her computer, her heart pounding. What had she just done?

EVIE WALKED up the long gravel driveway toward the very top of the property. She loved the view from up here. Of course, her mother was always watching her like a hawk lately, after her little excursion to the creek led her to an unintended overnight stay in the woods and a sprained ankle. But, at least she had a killer story to tell.

Then again, who would she tell?

She had no friends in Carter's Hollow, and all of her so-called friends back home had all but forgotten she even existed. The first few weeks she was at the B&B, they'd been in touch on text. Then, their correspondence had been reduced to social media and the occasional direct message. Now, she watched them all from afar, wondering if they were ever truly her friends anyway.

She'd always had a tough time trusting people. After all, her own father had abandoned her, and her mother had spent the last few years continually angry at her for one thing or another. Even her teachers glared at her with an intensity that should've been reserved for serial killers and people who don't recycle.

Being at the B&B and getting to know her aunt had made her feel calmer than she had in years. She was starting to belong somewhere, even if it was out in the middle of the Georgia woods.

Nature had never been her thing, but now she enjoyed her hikes, even though most of them were only to the end of the driveway and back. Her mother had approved of those sorts of walks, as long as Evie had a fully charged phone and agreed not to veer off course.

Lately, her mother was much more occupied with her budding new relationship. Cooper seemed nice enough. He certainly carried her up that ravine after she'd fallen a couple of weeks back, so she gave him credit for that. But, there was a part of her that was jealous of the time her mother was now spending on the business and Cooper. She sometimes worried she'd get replaced just like her father replaced her with a whole new family.

As she reached the top of the driveway, she climbed up into her favorite tree. It was a big oak with low hanging limbs, perfect for climbing. It was also the best spot she'd found to stare out over the blue hued mountains and dream about the future.

Maybe she would become a nurse and try to help people. Although she really hated needles, and the smell of the hospital made her want to vomit.

Maybe she would travel the world as a nature photographer. But she really wasn't all that fond of airplanes, and the thought of getting eaten by a lion out in the middle of the jungle somewhere made her cringe.

Or maybe she would stay right here, on this land that made her feel like she was at home. Maybe she would help her aunt Mia run the B&B. For some reason, even at her young age, the thought of that didn't make her too uncomfortable.

While most of her friends back in Rhode Island had these big plans for their lives - usually traveling or going to some Ivy League college - she ached for roots. For family.

She leaned back against the sturdy wood and closed her eyes, her legs dangling on either side of the limb, lightly swaying in the breeze.

This would be her first fall in the mountains, but she was looking forward to it. It was still "as hot as blue blazes", as her Aunt Mia would say, since it was only mid August. But she was looking forward to seeing the leaves change color and then eventually fall from the trees, revealing more of the mountains surrounding them.

But then there would be school. Next month, in fact. Her mother had already been talking about going back to Rhode Island soon so that she could get on with her studies, but Evie had pushed back, saying that she didn't want to go back there for school. There was nothing left for her in Rhode Island. Beautiful as it was there, she didn't want to go back.

For now, they had agreed to table the argument for at least another week. She told her mother that she would rather do school online then go back to Rhode Island and leave her new life behind.

A part of her had to admit that she missed having friends. Her so-called friends in Rhode Island had never been all that great. In fact, many of them were the top troublemakers in the school. Nobody popular wanted to hang around with her. She had been the oddball, stuck on the fringes of school society since she'd hit middle school.

Evie had always been a bit of a conundrum to those around her. Her personality shifted from angry to good natured in a split second, sometimes even surprising her. And her desire to constantly find herself in troubling situations wasn't something that most people wanted to be a part of, unless, of course, they liked to get into trouble too.

But she missed having people her age around. Being

around grownups all the time was often boring. The thought of going to a brand new school in a brand new state scared her, but a part of her found it exciting. She would get to meet all new people, none of whom knew anything about her past. Nobody would know all the trouble she'd gotten into. Nobody would know all the times she was in detention or had to redo a class just to keep from failing the grade she was in.

And nobody would know that she had been abandoned by her own father.

Every time she thought about him, she wanted to cry. When she was little, she had been such a daddy's girl. They would sometimes throw the ball together in the front yard, with her father saying that he wished he had a son. When he would say that, it would hurt her feelings, but she never said anything. She just tried to be the best baseball player she could, often practicing against the side of their house, throwing a tennis ball at the brick over and over again when her dad was at work.

She had always wanted to impress him. But it never seemed to be enough, and the moment he could bolt and leave her stranded, he did. He built a whole new family, including a little boy, proving to her once again that she just didn't matter much.

Of course, her mother was different. Kate had tried everything to keep her daughter in line, and Evie appreciated it, even when she acted like she didn't. She knew that her mother was doing everything possible to give her a good life, including coming all the way to

Georgia to give her another family member who cared about her.

She leaned back against the tree again, taking a deep breath of the mountain air, thick and hot as it was.

Just as she was dozing off against the trunk behind her, she heard a crack. Thinking it might be the limb she was sitting on, she immediately bolted upright, looking down at where she was sitting, trying to assess the situation. What would she latch onto if the whole thing fell? She wasn't exactly the outdoorsy type just yet, so she didn't have an idea in her head on what to do if she started falling towards the earth at a rapid clip.

When she realized that her limb wasn't moving, she looked around, surveying the rest of the tree. Maybe a limb was about to fall on top of her. As she looked up and in front of her, she saw another pair of feet dangling from the tree. Startled, she put her hand on her chest, her breath stuck in her throat.

"Hey! Who's up there?" she called, the familiar hint of anger in her voice.

She heard a deep voice respond, obviously that of a boy whose voice had recently changed. "A better question is who's down there?"

She looked up again, noticing only a pair of dirty white Converse tennis shoes dangling there, the sun obscuring his face and only showing a dark silhouette.

"I live on this property. And you happen to be in *my* tree, so I think you should answer me first!"

"Do you have a survey to prove where your property ends and mine begins?"

"No. That would be stupid."

Without warning, he suddenly started shimmying down the tree, landing on another thick limb right beside hers. She cut her eyes over at him, unable to keep herself from looking. He was a teenage boy, after all, and she had newly acquired hormones that prevented her from not noticing a good looking guy.

And he was good looking. Scruffy, but cute. Hair longer than it should've been, a dirty brown color. Fuller lips. Light colored eyes. An oversized pair of khaki shorts, not the most fashionable. A band T-shirt for some group she'd never heard of, but cool in the fashion sense.

"What's your name?" he asked. Boy, this guy was direct.

"None of your business."

He leaned forward, reaching out his hand. "Hi, none of your business. Nice to meet you."

She cut her eyes at him again and then rolled them, not taking his hand, even though she wanted to.

"You're a regular comedian."

"I'm also polite. I can tell you're not from around here. And by the way, my name is Dustin."

"I didn't ask." She sighed. "Fine. My name is Evie. And I live at Sweet Tea B&B."

"Oh, wow. Then you must know Miss Mia."

Evie laughed. "She's my aunt."

"I've got to say I'm surprised that Miss Mia would have relatives from up north."

Evie rolled her eyes again. "Well, she does. And I'd still like to know why you're in my tree?"

He leaned back against the trunk, his feet dangling just like hers. "I like to come up here. It's the best view in the whole area."

She had to agree with him on that. As soon as she had found this perch, she decided to come here every day, weather permitting. For some reason, it just calmed her down.

"But you shouldn't go on other people's property."

Dustin laughed. "Around here, we share the land. Miss Mia wouldn't care that I'm up here. She knows my momma."

"I'm sure she does. Well, I need to get back to the house. I can see that my quiet place has been invaded."

She climbed down, gingerly, being sure not to fall in front of the new guy. Even though he annoyed her, he was cute, and there was no reason to fall flat on her face in front of him.

"Hey!" he called as she started down the gravel road.

"What?" she said, hands on her hips as she looked up at him.

"It's nice to meet you. See you tomorrow?"

She laughed under her breath, shook her head and turned back toward the house. She wanted to tell him no, but there was a really good chance she would be seeing him tomorrow.

CHAPTER 2

*M*ia checked her email for the third time in as many hours before slamming the laptop shut. Why had she opened herself up to this man, her biological father, to disappoint her? She had been just fine before finding out the information that there had been yet another DNA match.

She stood up and walked toward the kitchen, feeling antsy. It wasn't yet time to start dinner, and she hadn't seen Kate or Evie in the last few hours. Last she heard, Evie had gone for a walk, and she didn't know where Kate had wandered off to.

Sometimes, she hated being alone with her thoughts. Most of the time, she found herself thinking about her mother and missing her. Some days were better than others, especially those where she found herself distracted with new guests or learning new things about Kate and Evie. Quiet times were the hardest.

Even harder was that she didn't have someone to

share her life with. Sure, she had her new sister and niece, but she hadn't seriously dated anyone in years.

And if she was honest with herself, watching Kate and Cooper start to fall in love made her a little envious. She was happy for them, but she wanted to be happy for herself also.

She walked upstairs, intent on going in her room and sulking for a while, but when she got into the hallway, she looked at the one door she never opened. The one that had been closed for months now. Her mother's private office.

Because of the size of the house, her mother had been able to have her own office space, more like a mini library. She had loved to read more than just about anyone Mia had ever met. A few years back, she'd had custom shelving installed all around the office and filled every square inch with all of her favorite books. If there was one thing Mia was sure of, it was that getting her mother books for every holiday was a safe bet.

But since she had passed away, Mia had not entered her office. She just couldn't bring herself to do it. Not only were all of her mother's books in there, but she knew the smell of her would hang in the air. She knew the feeling of her mother would loft over her the second she walked in the door. And while that might have been a welcome thought to most people, for her it was agonizing. To be able to feel her mother but not touch her or talk to her or hug her seemed like a devastating prospect.

There was a part of her, though, that wanted to

walk through that door, to feel her presence and touch her things. She knew that her mother kept private keepsakes in boxes in the closet inside of the office, but Mia had never gone through them. It was upsetting enough finding all of those journals that only mentioned the time that she was pregnant with Kate. Somewhere, there had to be journals about Mia's early moments of life. Maybe her mother just didn't want her to know her origins.

Many times, she thought about what her birth father must've been like. Had she been a product of rape? Had it been a one night stand? She shook the thought out of her head, knowing her mother wasn't that kind of woman. She loved hard, and she wouldn't have gotten pregnant on a whim.

Even her pregnancy with Kate seemed to be brought about from love. Not knowing how her story began left a strange void in Mia's heart that she didn't know if she would ever fill.

Maybe that was one of the reasons why she hadn't had a successful adult relationship. Her ability to trust wavered at times, not really knowing how to build a solid relationship. She'd never seen her mom and dad together, holding hands while sitting on the sofa on a Friday night watching TV. She hadn't experienced it, so she didn't really know what that was like.

"Are you okay?" Kate asked from behind her. She had been so lost in thought that she hadn't even heard her sister walking behind her on the hardwood floor.

"Yeah. I was just… reminiscing, I guess."

Kate walked up beside her and stared in the direction that Mia was looking. "What's behind that door?"

Mia blew out a breath. "That's Momma's private office. I just haven't been able to make myself walk through those doors since she died."

Kate put her arm around Mia's shoulders and squeezed. "Are you thinking about going in now?"

"I don't know. One minute I think I'm ready and the next I want to run straight out into the hills back there."

Kate smiled. "You know, big sisters are here for things like this. Why don't we do it together?"

Mia thought for one moment longer. "Okay."

She regretted it as soon as she said it, but she decided it was time. Something about that office was calling her, just like her momma was telling her from heaven that it was okay to start moving on.

They approached the door, and Mia stopped. "You know, a lot of times when somebody dies, It's like they were never here. The generations just move on, and before you know it nobody even remembers that person. I don't want that to happen to Momma. She was too special. And I think generations after us should remember her, but I don't know how to make that happen."

Kate nodded. "We'll figure it out. One step at a time."

Mia nodded before reaching down and turning the door handle.

≈

LEARNING how to be a good big sister was something Kate never thought she'd be faced with, especially at her age. Pushing forty, she'd never imagined that she would be standing in the doorway of her birth mother's office with her brand new sister, wondering how to support her through the grief of losing their mother.

Reading her mother's journals had given her insight into who she was and how she felt in one of the worst times of her young life. But, she couldn't grieve the way Mia was. And, in a way, that gave her a whole different type of grief to deal with on her own. How did she grieve someone she never got to meet?

It wasn't only that she didn't get to meet her mother. She'd never even known she existed until recently. Her entire life had been a lie, with her parents making her believe that she was biologically theirs. Sometimes, she thought about speaking with a counselor, just to work through the hurt feelings she carried for the parents who raised her.

She had suffered through thinking her father had abandoned her, and he had, but it turned out he wasn't her biological father. There were so many lies that had been woven throughout the fabric of her life that it was hard to grieve each one. And still, there was a lot of anger there.

Right now, her focus had to be on her sister. Going into their mother's office months after her death was difficult for Mia. She had memories and experiences with her mother that Kate never would, so she couldn't fully understand the depth and breadth of Mia's grief as they walked through the door.

The office was lighter and brighter than Kate had imagined. With custom white bookshelves built into the walls and bright pink and white upholstery on the small settee near the window, it looked like something out of an interior design magazine.

Much more floral than Kate would've liked, the office was full of life, but at the same time full of death. Mia just stood there, her arms hanging by her side like two limp spaghetti noodles, her head slightly hanging. Kate could hear her taking a deep breath.

"It still smells like her. Do you smell that perfume? She always put on too much," Mia said, laughing sadly. "I used to tell her that she stayed in a room for hours after she left it."

Kate smiled. "I smell it. I guess I know what my mother smells like now."

Mia turned and smiled at her. "I guess you do. I'm so sorry you never got to know her."

"Me too. So, where would you like to start?"

"Look at all these books. I know most people have shelves full of books that they never read, but Momma read every one of these, some of them twice."

"She sounds like a very smart woman."

"She was," Mia said, laughing. "She often surprised people, you know. Being so southern and sweet, people automatically thought she was stupid. But she wasn't. She was more well read then anyone I've ever met."

"I bet she was. People who read this many books have to be pretty smart."

"I just don't know what to do with all of them. I

can't just throw them away. One time she told me she'd haunt me for such a thing."

Kate chuckled. "Well, as much as I'd like to meet her, I really don't need a ghost haunting this place, so let's not do that."

Mia walked over to her mother's desk, the tips of her fingers trailing along the dark wood, as she stared down at the organized chaos below.

"She had way too much paperwork. I don't even know what most of this stuff is. I tried to get her to do everything on the computer, but she barely turned it on. It just wasn't her thing."

"I can see that."

"I bought her a really fancy phone a couple of years ago, but she refused to get rid of her flip phone. Never even knew how to send a text," Mia said, reminiscing.

"Well, there's something to be said for doing things in the old-school way. I wish Evie would stop staring at her phone so much. Kids these days miss out on a lot of life experiences."

"They sure do." Mia sat down in her mother's very plush, black leather chair. The hardwood floor creaked below it as she sat down. She looked around the desktop and then smiled as she picked up a shiny, royal blue pen. "This was Momma's favorite pen. I remember when Bobby bought it for her. These things are very expensive, and she tried to get him to take it back. But he wasn't having any of that. Told her that she was worth a thousand of these pens. She wouldn't write with anything else, especially after he died."

"I'm glad she had a second chance at love."

Mia tilted her head and looked at her sister. "Maybe a third chance? I mean, I'm hoping she was in love with my father and yours."

Kate sat down in the chair across from the desk. "Do you think so? I mean, I guess we'll find out when you hear from your father."

"You mean *if* I hear from him. He hasn't messaged me back."

"Mia, it hasn't been that long," Kate said, laughing as she shook her head. "Maybe you get your impatient streak from him."

"Maybe so, although Momma was very impatient. Poor Bobby was always running late, and I remember she used to pick at him about that. It was her biggest pet peeve, aside from somebody putting down a drink without a coaster."

Kate laughed. "I must get that from her. I do the same thing."

Mia looked around the room and sighed. "I don't know how I'll ever go through all of this stuff."

"You don't have to do it alone, and you don't have to do it all at once. This stuff isn't going anywhere."

"I know that Momma would want me to turn this room into something to benefit the bed-and-breakfast. But, I just don't know if I can bring myself to do it."

"Why can't we just use it for our own office? We could put another little desk over here, or take the one out of the living room."

"Maybe. Or we could create some kind of library for the guests."

Kate shook her head. "I don't think our guests need

a library. They aren't coming to Sweet Tea B&B to read, Mia."

"Momma believed that reading was the best kind of relaxation."

"I know, but we need an office. It would make much more sense for us to use it for that," Kate said, worried that they might be having their second argument as sisters, the first one having been in the attorney's office.

"We have time to think about it," Mia said, obviously not wanting to start an argument. "What's that?"

She stood up and walked over to the corner of the room. There was a door, probably to a closet, with a small piece of fabric sticking out of it. She opened the door.

"Wow. I haven't seen this jacket since I was a kid."

She pulled out a bright pink raincoat, the size that a little girl would've worn. She held it up and smiled.

"I remember when Momma surprised me with this. I think I was going into the fourth grade, and another little girl in class had a coat like this. We barely had any money at the time, but somehow she managed to scrape it together and buy me this coat. I just remember being so proud to wear it to school and thinking that one day I would give it to my little girl, but that never happened."

"You still have plenty of time," Kate said, putting her hand on Mia's shoulder.

"No, I do believe my ship has sailed. I just forgot to get on it."

Kate chuckled. "Your prince charming is out there somewhere."

Mia looked at her sister. "I don't think he's going to find me way out in the woods hiding at a bed-and-breakfast, do you?"

Kate shrugged her shoulders. "Who knows? Stranger things have happened. I mean, I'm dating Cooper."

Mia laughed "You're right. Strange things definitely *do* happen."

THE TRUCK CAME TO A STOP. Kate sat there, picnic basket in her lap, and waited for Cooper to come around and open the door. If there was anything she had learned about true southern gentlemen, it was that they always opened the door. She'd given up even reaching for the handle at this point.

The slightly feminist part of her wanted to be offended, but she wasn't. She knew he didn't open doors and walk closest to the street because he was being disrespectful. In fact, he was respecting her and trying to protect her, and she thought it was kind of cute.

He opened the door, and she stepped down, his hand on her lower back. "So are you ready for the long-awaited picnic?"

Kate smiled. "Yes, I am. And I'm curious what I'm going to find in this picnic basket you brought."

He took it from her and grinned. "I'm actually a pretty good little cook, I'll have you know."

They started walking toward the trail, the last slivers of sunlight peeking through the trees. In true Cooper fashion, he was honoring her request to have a moonlit dinner on the deck overlooking the river and waterfall on his clients' land.

"And you're sure they don't mind us being down here?"

Cooper laughed. "I'm positive. Now, come on," he reached over and took her hand as they made their way down the incline to the overlook deck.

Something about his hand in hers made everything all right. As much as she didn't want to rely on anyone, especially a man, she couldn't seem to help herself. He was stable and strong and kind. Every time she let herself start to feel that way again, she flashed back to her marriage with Brandon. There was a moment where she thought he was some of those things too. Trust is a hard thing.

When they reached the deck, Cooper set the picnic basket on the table and then took both of her hands, pulling her over to the edge. "Take a look at that." He pointed off in the distance, where the pink sky, streaked by the last remnants of daylight, shone over the edge of the rocks and trees in the distance.

"It's beautiful. We have some pretty areas in Rhode Island, but nothing like this."

"Yeah, the beauty of these mountains isn't something I've seen anywhere else."

"Have you done a lot of traveling?" Kate asked,

turning toward him, her elbow leaning against the deck rail.

"Actually, I did. For a couple of years I just sort of traveled around trying to get my head on straight, I guess. Got to visit Mexico, New York City, Texas."

"Wow, those are nowhere near each other," she said with a laugh.

"Well, I did do a little visiting in places in between. I had a rough go for a couple of years, so I was kind of floating around out there."

"Mind if I ask what happened?"

He turned and leaned his forearms against the deck and stared out over the mountains like he was a million miles away.

"I was married, and things didn't work out."

"Been there, done that, burned the T-shirt in a fit of rage."

Cooper laughed. "It can really do a number on your head, can't it?"

"Very true. And it wouldn't be so bad except my despicable ex went off and started a whole new family and left his daughter behind."

Cooper shook his head. "I guess I should be glad we didn't have any kids between us, because I can't imagine how difficult that would have been. But there's no way I would've left my kid for any reason. I'm sorry that you and Evie have to deal with that."

Kate sighed. "Yeah, it's hard, but it's so much worse for her. A girl needs her father. I'm so worried about her future relationships because she doesn't know what a real man acts like."

"I think she'll be okay. She's got a great mother," Cooper said, smiling over at her. Why was it that men with dimples were so much more handsome?

"Thanks. It's been a rough few years with her becoming a teenager. We were so much closer when she was a little girl and I could control everything. Now, I found out that I have raised a stubborn, hardheaded woman."

Cooper chuckled. "The apple doesn't fall far…"

Kate held up a finger. "It's best that you don't finish that sentence." He smiled, that all too attractive dimple cropping up yet again.

"To save me from you pushing me off this mountain, why don't we go ahead and start eating?"

"Good plan," she said with a laugh.

She followed him over to the picnic table and sat down. As he opened the basket, she was amazed at what she saw. Assuming he would just bring sandwiches, she was pleasantly surprised when he pulled out containers that were covered, steam rising from inside of them.

"What is all of this?"

"I made my famous garlic chicken with cheesy mashed potatoes and homemade yeast rolls."

"Seriously?"

"Listen, my momma was an amazing cook. And since she had a bunch of boys, we were all forced to learn how to cook. I guess it's finally paying off."

"I guess so," she said, smiling over at him. As they started to eat, she was amazed at how easy the conversation went. He regaled her with tales of growing up in the mountains while she told him all of her worst experiences doing party planning for rich people.

"So, this louse of an ex husband of yours, how long has it been since Evie has seen him?"

"Years. He doesn't even send her a birthday card."

"What a jerk."

"How about you? Do you ever hear from your ex?" She didn't know why she was asking other than just morbid curiosity.

"No. In fact, she's married now, for the third time, and lives somewhere in Washington from what I hear."

"Can I ask why any woman would leave you when you can cook like this?"

He smiled. "Apparently my ability to make strawberry shortcake was not enough to keep her from cheating on me with my best friend."

Her eyes widened. "Okay, we're going to have to come back to the strawberry shortcake because I'm going to need to know more about that. But, she cheated with your best friend? Is he still around?"

"No. I kicked him to the curb also. It was a really rough time in my life, to realize that I had nobody I could trust."

She took another bite of her roll, wishing he brought more but not wanting to gorge herself and look like some sort of pig. "I understand. I had always been pretty trusting, but Brandon shattered that into a million pieces."

"It took me a long time to realize that not every woman was like my ex. And not every friend is like my former best friend. People are people, nobody is the same. At some point, I realized that I just have to give people a chance and that sometimes it's worth trusting someone, even if it's a little scary."

She took a sip of her sweet tea, still getting used to the taste of it. "I guess you're right. Although, I'm not sure I'm there yet. Anyone who wants to get close to me is going to have to climb up quite a wall."

She said it more as a warning, wondering if it would scare him off.

"Well, then, I guess it's a good thing I have strong legs and arms made for climbing," he said with a wink.

Something about that statement gave her a tingle.

CHAPTER 3

*M*ia stood outside watering her garden.
Her mother had always wanted to have
a big garden on the property, but they'd always been so
busy and never had the time. Now, all Mia had was
time. With the additional help of her sister, she could
finally take a breath and know that she wasn't alone in
running the B&B. At least, temporarily. Who knew
how long Kate would agree to stay?

As she drizzled water over her new plants – collard
greens, different types of lettuce and broccoli - she
thought about what it was going to be like if Kate and
Evie ever left. She'd become very accustomed to them
being there.

Kate had talked a lot in recent weeks about what
she was going to do with Evie and school. One option
was to take her back to Rhode Island, but there was a
very good chance that the school she had attended
wouldn't take her back anyway. That would leave Kate

in the lurch trying to find a private school that she could afford.

Selfishly, Mia hoped Kate would stay there and put Evie in the local public school. But she didn't want to push, even though she secretly prayed every night that they would stay.

As she finished her watering, she pressed the button on the garden hose dispenser to roll it up. It came flying at her with a force she wasn't expecting, the tail end of it, heavy and metal, almost knocking her right in the face. Thankfully, she was alone and her new guests weren't arriving until the evening, or that would've been quite embarrassing.

"Excuse me?" a man said from behind her. She froze in place. Nobody was supposed to be there. Kate was in town, Evie was out on one of her grand adventures in the woods, and Cooper only came around when Kate was there.

She slowly turned, and her legs almost gave way when she saw who it was.

"Travis?" she stammered, dropping her gardening gloves onto the ground beside her.

"Hey, Mia. It's so good to see you," he said, that familiar, lazy smile spreading across his face. She remembered that smile very well.

"What on earth are you doing here? The last I heard, you were living in San Diego."

"I came back to visit my mom and dad. Dad's not doing very well."

She had loved his parents at one time. Mia had heard around town that his father had some health problems, and she occasionally saw his mother in passing on the town square, both of them keeping their distance.

"I'm sorry to hear that. I know how difficult that is. But why are you here, at the B&B?"

"I guess because I wanted to see you."

She laughed, more out of irony than humor, and shook her head. "After all these years? Not a phone call or a text or letter, even when my momma died? Now you want to see me?"

"Now, Mia, that's not fair…"

She put her hand up. "Let's not do this. There's no need to rehash things that happened long ago. I just don't understand why you're standing here right now."

"Well, I sort of have a room reserved here for the next week or so."

"What? Why aren't you staying with your parents?"

"Like I said, Daddy isn't doing well. Me coming and going all the time would disrupt him resting, and we have other family in town that are using the guest room…"

"Look, Travis, I'm sorry. Your daddy is a good man, and I'm so glad that you're here for him. But you absolutely cannot stay here."

"Mia, you know as well as I do that there's nowhere else to stay in this town. I need to be near my parents in case Mom needs to call me. If I have to stay another town over, I might miss… Well, I might miss the end of my father's life. Are you really going to hold a grudge and keep me from seeing my daddy before he dies?"

She sighed, knowing exactly what that felt like. If

she hadn't been there when her mother took her last breath, she never would've forgiven herself.

"Fine. But let's make one thing clear, Travis. We're not friends. We're not even acquaintances anymore. You're simply a guest at my B&B."

"Agreed." She walked past him. Travis followed along behind her as they walked around the front of the house and up to the front porch. "

"I'll get you checked in if you want to grab your luggage."

He nodded and turned toward his car. As Mia watched him walk away, she couldn't believe that Travis Norton was standing on her property. There was nothing else that would've shocked her more, even if a meteor came crashing out of the sky and hit her in the head right now.

RAVEN'S MOUTH HUNG OPEN, her fork in mid air with a dollop of potato salad leaning over the edge dangerously.

"So you're telling me that Travis Norton is back in Carter's Hollow?"

Mia nodded. "You could've knocked me over with a feather when I saw him. Imagine me just watering my plants and then I turn around and see him standing there."

Raven ate her bite of food and shook her head. "You have plants now?"

"I'm growing a garden."

"Girl, you've never had a green thumb," Raven said, laughing.

"Okay, can we get back on topic? Travis Norton was standing in my yard!"

"So what is he doing here?"

"His father is ill. He wanted to come back here to be close to him in his final days."

"That's sad. I always liked his father."

"Me too," Mia said with a sigh. "And he's staying at the B&B."

Again, Raven's mouth dropped open, and this time she dropped a chunk of potato salad right on her white T-shirt. Groaning, she wiped it off and then looked back at Mia.

"Why on earth are you going to let him stay there? You know that's dangerous territory, Mia."

"Trust me, I know. But there's no room for him at his parents' house, and you know we're the only place to stay in town. I felt bad telling him to stay outside of town, so far away from his dad."

"You were always too good to him."

Mia took a long sip of her tea, and then leaned her head over onto one hand.

"I have to admit, as soon as I saw him, those butter-flies came right back."

Raven reached across and squeezed Mia's hand. "You know that's not smart. He broke your heart."

"He was just the first in a long line of heartbreaks, Raven."

"We both know he was the hardest one."

"It was just young love."

Raven leaned back in her chair and crossed her arms. "You realize who you're talking to, right?"

"It was a long time ago."

"Have you been practicing all of these statements? Travis was the love of your life, and he just about broke you."

"We were in high school. That was ages ago."

"You can keep saying that, but I see the look on your face. You're playing with fire letting him stay there."

"I'm just going to do my very best to stay away from him."

Raven laughed. "And how are you going to do that when you run the bed-and-breakfast?"

"Well, I don't run it alone anymore. I'll just make sure that Kate is the one interacting with him as much as possible."

"Sure, that will totally work."

"You know, you could try supporting me," Mia said.

"You know I'll support you until the ends of the earth, but I hate to see you go into something and get your heart broken all over again."

Mia rolled her eyes. "Travis Norton is simply a guest at my B&B. Nothing more."

"I hope you're right."

KATE STOOD behind the welcome desk and smiled. It wasn't really in her nature to be this interactive with people. That's why she had enjoyed party planning because she got to be behind the scenes. But helping to run the B&B meant that she had to be the face of the place, and smiling was a new part of her job.

"Welcome to our B&B. We're glad to have you here. Can I get your name please?"

It wasn't like they had a whole slate of people checking in. The only person staying there had moved in that morning. Mia had told Kate who he was and how much she needed to avoid him, and so far that seemed to be working. Kate had done everything she could to make sure that Mia didn't run into Travis. But that also meant that Mia was eating dinner in her room.

"Our reservation is under Sylvia and Jack Townsend."

The couple seemed nice enough, but their demeanor was a little bit strange. Sylvia seemed jumpy, darting her eyes around the room like she was about to get caught for shoplifting. Jack, on the other hand, seemed completely disinterested.

"Oh yes, I see you right here. You're going to be in room four. Here's your key. Let me show you to your room," Kate said, walking toward the stairs.

The quiet nature of this couple was a little off-putting, even for Kate. She expected some sort of inter-action or excitement when people came to visit the B&B. After all, it was out in the middle of nowhere, and most people who had traveled a long time to get there. But these two didn't seem like they wanted to be there at all.

"Here we are. There's a communal bathroom here across the hall. Just make sure to flip the sign when you're in there so no one accidentally walks in. Sometimes that lock doesn't operate correctly."

"The lock doesn't work?" Jack said.

"Only occasionally. Just make sure you really hear it click," Kate said, plastering on a smile. They had to get that lock fixed. She made a mental note to text Cooper about that later. Any excuse to see him.

She opened the door to their room, revealing one of her favorite spaces in the house. It was decorated in more of a French country style, something she had always liked.

"This is your room. If you need anything, extra towels or shampoo, you can just dial zero on the phone. Or you can come downstairs and tell us, of course. Dinner is at seven o'clock every night. Breakfast is at seven AM. If you have any special dietary needs, be sure to let us know, and we will do our best to accommodate you."

She had memorized the little speech she was supposed to give, although when Mia did it, there was a lot more southern flair and silly jokes.

"Thank you. I think we'll just settle in for a while and see you at dinner," Sylvia said, making it very clear she wanted Kate to make a quick exit.

"Of course. I think tonight we're having pot roast, one of our guests' favorites. I hope you'll join us."

As she made her way out of the room, she had a funny feeling. There was something about this couple that was just a little bit off, but who was she to judge?

As long as they paid their bill and and didn't try to murder anyone, she would just let them be.

SYLVIA UNZIPPED HER SUITCASE, pulling out a stack of shirts. She turned and put them in the top drawer of the dresser.

"I still don't understand why we came all the way here. What's so special about this place?" Jack asked, looking out the front window.

"You don't think it's beautiful here?"

He turned around and crossed his arms. "Come on, Sylvia. You know as well as I do that we don't come to places like this. Why did you bring me here?"

Sylvia walked over and put her arms around his waist looking up at him. "Because I thought it would be nice to get away for a while. You're always working. I saw this place in a magazine, and it looked quaint and out-of-the-way. I doubt we can even get cell service here."

He squinted his eyes, obviously still unsure of her motivation. "You normally like fancy hotels and room service. Now we're going to eat pot roast with strangers out in the woods. That just doesn't seem like you."

"Besides, didn't you grow up somewhere around here?"

"Yes, and I left a long time ago. This place has a lot of memories I prefer not to recall."

"Are you ever going to tell me about those memories?" she asked, rubbing her thumb across one of his cheeks.

"Some memories are better left in the past."

He had said the same thing a million times before in their twenty years of marriage. No matter how many times she tried to get him to open up, he would shut it down almost as quickly.

There was so much about her husband that she didn't know, so many questions she wanted to ask but knew she wouldn't get answers to.

If he only knew why she brought him here. She was deceiving him, and she hated it, but she had to know for sure. She had to understand where he came from and what he left behind.

"I think we're going to have a nice time. You've been working really hard for a long time, Jack. Let's just take some time to enjoy being together. Besides, I know you can't wait to throw your fishing line in that lake out there."

He smiled slightly. "I haven't fished in a couple of decades."

She walked across the room and picked up his fishing pole. "No time like the present."

EVIE COULDN'T BELIEVE IT. Somehow she had convinced her mother to let her stay and enroll in school. As much as she hated school, it was certainly better to stay in Carter's Hollow than go back to Rhode Island and face all of the demons of her past.

This was a new start, and she was determined to make the most of it. Maybe she would actually make friends, for once. Maybe people wouldn't judge her for not having a dad or for being rebellious. Maybe she would be able to start fresh.

"I don't know where we're supposed to go. Is it down that hallway, or that one?" her mother asked, staring down at a printed map in her hand. "

"I don't know. I've never been here either," Mia said, looking back-and-forth.

For such a small town, everybody who lived there seemed to be inside of the high school right now. And everybody seemed to know each other.

Kids were running all directions, hugging each other after a long summer apart. Teachers were smiling and waving, parents were greeting each other with handshakes.

Evie already felt a little bit out of place. She didn't know anyone. Well, maybe except for the boy she met in the tree the other day. She wasn't even sure he went to this high school.

"Tree girl?" he said, as if on cue, from behind her.

Kate turned, cocking her head to the side. "Tree girl?"

Evie rolled her eyes. "Mom, this is Dustin. We met for a brief moment in the tree that I sit in on the property."

Kate smiled and reached out her hand to shake Dustin's. "Oh. Very nice. Good to meet you, Dustin."

"Good to meet you too, ma'am."

"Say, Dustin, do you happen to know where we can find the registration area?"

"Sure. Just take a left down this hallway. You should see it at the very end."

"Great. Come along, Evie."

"See ya," Dustin said, winking at Evie before trotting off down another hallway.

She followed her mother to the registration area. There was a long line.

"Do you mind if I go walk around a little bit? I want to get an idea of where I'm going."

"But you don't even know your schedule yet."

"I just want to see where everything is, Mom. I'll meet up with you in the front of the school in a little while. Just text me."

"Fine. But be watching your phone," Kate said, a warning tone in her voice.

Evie nodded and then walked away. As she made her way around the school, she tried to memorize all of the spaces. The last thing she needed was to get lost on her first day and be the one late for class that everyone would stare at when she walked in the door.

She found the gymnasium, complete with basket-ball court and bleachers. It was smaller than her high school back in Rhode Island, but still pretty nice.

Around the corner from that was the science lab and then the library. It was way smaller than the one she was used to, but then she wasn't one to go check out books anyway.

Finally, she found the cafeteria. It was about the

same size as the one at her high school with the same long, boring brown tables that had the attached seats.

The high school she had gone to in Rhode Island had all different types of food with little windows for each. There was international, the pizza station and even one for vegetarian kids. Nobody ever got anything from that area.

This cafeteria was much less formal or complex. There was one line for everything, so she hoped that she liked the food. If not, she might be begging her aunt Mia to pack her lunch every day.

She walked over to one of the tables and sat down. Everybody was milling about, chatting around the room. Some parents were signing their kids up for lunch card while others were catching up with old friends.

"Fancy meeting you here," Dustin said as he plopped down beside her.

"Geez, are you my stalker now?"

"You know, you might be nice to me since I seem to be your only friend in town."

"Oh, you're my friend now? I literally met you in a tree for like thirty seconds."

"Have you met any other people in trees lately?"

She rolled her eyes. "No. Just you, unfortunately."

"Listen, I'm well loved at this school. I've been living here my entire life, and every parent, teacher and student knows me."

She stared at him. "Are you running for office or something?"

"No. But I would win. Totally."

She shook her head. "I don't think I've ever met anyone as ridiculously cocky as you are. And that's not a compliment." She stood up and started walking back toward the hallway. Dustin jumped up and followed her.

"Okay, fine. Maybe I'm overly confident. But, you're new at the school, right?"

Evie continued to walk. "You know that I am."

"Well, I'd like to introduce you to some of my friends. You don't want to start school and not know anyone, do you?"

She didn't know what his motivation was, and she questioned it. But there was another part of her that wanted to know people before she started school. She didn't want to be that weird girl that nobody knew.

"Let's just say that I'm interested in meeting some friends. What exactly are you getting at?"

"We're having a back to school party this weekend. A bunch of us are going to meet up over at Miller's Point."

"Miller's Point?"

"It's one of the coves on the lake. There's a big cave over there, and we do bonfires. It's also near the old water tower."

"I think I know where the water tower is."

"Good. Be there Friday night, seven o'clock. BYOB."

"Beer? I'm 15 years old."

"Not beer. Burger."

"Burger?"

"Everybody brings a pack of hamburger meat. It's a cookout. We cook over the fire."

Evie shook her head. "I don't understand this place."

Dustin laughed. "That's why I'm here to help you." He smiled one more time before trotting off again into the crowd.

She wasn't sure if this party was a good idea or not, but then again, she'd never been one for good ideas.

CHAPTER 4

*M*ia pulled the pot roast out of the oven, worried that she had let it cook a little too long. She liked the crunchy black edges, but the last thing she needed was for dinner to be as tough as shoe leather. She needed to get it on the table and get out of sight before she had an interaction with Travis.

Her history with him had been mostly beautiful, a high school romance for the ages. Never had anyone made her feel so loved and cared for, even at that young age.

Travis had great parents, a mom and dad who truly loved him. And they had welcomed her into their family from the very start.

For two years, they had dated, making plans for their future together. They would get married, have a passel of kids and sit in their rocking chairs one day.

And then Travis had changed his mind.

All throughout high school, his passion had been photography. He worked on the school newspaper and even did wedding photos on the side. He loved capturing the majesty of the Blue Ridge Mountains, and the beauty of the wildlife surrounding the area.

Many times, he had taken pictures of Mia, bemused by the way the light danced on all of the features of her face. She loved to spend time with him in the dark room his father had built for him off of their laundry room. It always amazed her how he saw things, how he could see the beauty in something that seemed so average at first glance, including herself. Teenage girls don't always have the best self confidence.

But then, he was offered a photography scholarship to school in New York City. She hadn't even known that he applied there, and suddenly he was leaving.

Their break up had been harder than anything she had gone through up until that point. Her mother had tried so hard to ease her broken heart, but not much helped. She wanted to be with him, and he wanted something else.

Knowing that she would never leave her mother, Travis left, cutting off all communication. She waited, checking the mailbox every day, hoping that he would send her a letter or postcard. She had hoped he would show up and say he made a mistake.

He never did.

It had been so many years since the day he drove away, and not once had she heard from him. Not one time. Not a Facebook message or a letter in the mail. Absolute radio silence.

That was what hurt the most. The years had only made it hurt worse, knowing that he had so easily moved on with his life. She imagined that he'd been traveling the globe all these years, taking pictures of rare flowers and dangerous wildlife. She imagined that he had dated a bunch of super models or gotten married to a beauty queen.

The truth was, she didn't know what his life had been like since high school, and she didn't want to know. All she knew was that when she looked at him, it brought back a level of pain she hadn't expected. It made her want to smack him across the face while simultaneously kissing those full lips of his.

Which was why she had to get dinner on the table and make a quick exit before she had any chance of running into him.

"Sorry I'm late," Kate said, as she came around the kitchen island. "School registration went way longer than I thought it would."

"I'm so glad you're letting Evie stay for school. I think she's really going to do well here," Mia said, stirring the mashed potatoes one more time.

"I hope so," Kate said, putting an apron over her head and then tying it behind her back. "Has Travis come down here yet?"

"No, which is why I want to get out of here as quickly as I can. I'm just going to make myself a plate and sneak up to my bedroom."

"How long can you keep this up?" Kate asked, taking the yeast rolls out of the oven.

"As long as I need to. He's staying here indefinitely, until something happens one way or the other with his father. There's really not much I can do to speed up that process, and I wouldn't want to. I actually like his father."

Kate smiled. "I think you like Travis too. And I think it's making you very uncomfortable."

"Well, thankfully I don't have time to get into all of the emotions of it. I just need to make my plate and…"

"Hey," Travis said from behind her.

Mia froze in place. Why had he come downstairs early? She hesitated to move, considering for a moment acting like one of those animals who didn't move as a way of making the other animal think it was dead. Would he buy that considering she was standing upright with her spoon firmly stuck into a bowl of mashed potatoes?

"Hi, Travis," Kate said, breaking the tension. "Dinner isn't for another fifteen minutes."

"I know. I'm sorry I came down early. It was just that I thought maybe I could offer to help out. Set the table or something?"

Mia turned around quickly. "We've got it. But thanks." She knew she was glaring at him, and she wanted to say that it was unintentional. But it wasn't. She'd been wanting to glare at Travis Norton for many years.

Evie, who had entered the room quietly, stood there. She stared at Mia and the man she was looking at.

"Hi. I'm Evie. You must be a new guest here?" she said, reaching out her dainty little hand.

"Hi. I'm Travis. I'll be staying here for a while. I'm an old friend of your aunt Mia's."

Mia laughed under her breath and turned back around to stir the mashed potatoes. They didn't require more stirring, but it was better than grabbing a butcher knife and flinging it across the kitchen at him.

"I think you're using the term friend rather loosely," Mia said quietly.

Kate cleared her throat. "You know what, Travis? I could actually use a hand setting the table, after all. Do you mind putting these plates over there? It will be the four of us plus two more."

She handed him a heavy stack of white restaurant ware plates and then turned back to Mia when he was out of earshot.

"Have you lost your mind? I'm not eating at the table with Travis."

Kate put her hands on Mia's shoulders. "Look, above all else, we have to be professional. We have two other guests staying with us right now, and they are kind of strange as it is. I am not going to be left down here with your old boyfriend and two very odd strangers by myself."

"You have Evie!" Mia said.

"Oh yes, my fifteen-year-old daughter is a wonderful conversationalist."

"Hey! I *am* a wonderful conversationalist!" Evie said.

"Fine! But I cannot be responsible for what I might blurt out during this meal." Mia took off her apron and wadded it up before tossing it on the counter.

"You have to be responsible. This is our business now, Mia. Do you really want our guests to think that you're a raving lunatic?"

"Not nice," Mia said, cutting her eyes up at Kate. She really hated that she was so tall sometimes.

"Look, I get it. This is very uncomfortable. But he's just a guest like any other guest. Don't let him get under your skin."

"Impossible," she said, rolling her eyes as she picked up the pot roast and walked over to the table.

A few minutes later, everyone had finally made their way into the kitchen. The new guests, Sylvia and Jack, sat on one side of the table with Mia and Kate at either end, and Travis and Evie on the other side. They were like one big, strange dysfunctional family.

"So, where did you guys come from?" Kate asked Sylvia as she took a bite of her potatoes.

Sylvia, looking uncomfortable for some reason, cleared her throat. "We actually live in Tennessee. Near Nashville."

"Beautiful area from what I hear. What do you do for a living?" Kate asked, trying to get some kind of conversation going at the table. At the moment, all she had to focus on was the fact that Mia kept staring at Travis, Travis kept staring at Mia and Evie looked like she was a rabbit caught in a trap between them.

"I work for a pharmaceutical company, and that's where I met Jack. He's the head of finance."

"Interesting," Kate said, knowing full well that it wasn't interesting. Nothing about pharmaceuticals or finance sounded very entertaining to her.

"It's actually not interesting at all," Jack said. She was surprised to hear his voice, deep and rough as it was. Very few people came through the B&B that were taller than Kate, but this guy towered above her by several inches.

"Then why do you do it?" Evie asked, in typical Evie fashion.

"Evie!" Kate said, shooting her a look.

"It's a good question," Jack said, smiling slightly. "Young lady, sometimes we make choices in life for other people instead of ourselves. It never leads anywhere good."

"Now, Jack, we've had a wonderful life together. We have a beautiful home, a nice boat..."

"Sylvia, having nice things has nothing to do with having an enjoyable life."

Looking uncomfortable again, Sylvia looked down, picked up her fork and filled her mouth with pot roast, obviously in an effort not to say anything further.

"So what brings you to Carter's Hollow?" Travis asked.

"Well, my wife brought me here, and I still don't really know why."

"I guess wives will do things like that sometimes," Travis said, laughing nervously.

"Oh? Is that how your wife is?" Mia asked, sarcasm dripping from her voice.

"I don't actually have a wife... anymore."

"Divorced?" Sylvia asked.

"Deceased," Travis said, looking down at his food.

Mia felt horrible. As much as she was mad at him, she didn't wish losing a loved one on anyone.

"I'm sorry to hear that," Mia said. Travis nodded slightly, and then looked down to continue eating.

"Jack was actually raised near here," Sylvia suddenly said. He looked at her, aggravation on his face.

"Oh yeah? Whereabouts?" Travis asked.

"Just a few towns over," Jack said, obviously not wanting to get into it.

"Mia, this pot roast is wonderful," Sylvia said.

"Thank you," she said. "It was my mother's recipe. She passed away recently."

"I'm so sorry to hear that. You must've been devastated."

"Yes, it's been very hard."

"And Kate, you're Mia's sister, right?"

"Yes, I am. But I didn't know our mother. She died before we found each other."

Sylvia cocked her head to the side. "Found each other?"

"We recently did our DNA testing online, and it connected us. We didn't know the other existed."

Sylvia's eyes widened, more so than a stranger just asking a simple question. It was odd.

"So... Do you have the same father?"

"Sylvia! That's none of your damn business," Jack said. He looked between Kate and Mia. "I'm so sorry. Sometimes she's a little too nosy for her own good."

"I'm sorry," Sylvia said.

"It's fine," Mia said, her southern hospitality showing. "We don't know our fathers. It's a long story."

The truth was, she didn't know any of the story. All she knew was that her mother was greatly in love with Kate's father, and her father didn't seem to exist.

The rest of the meal was rushed, with each of them

wanting to get up from the table. Mia couldn't remember a more awkward moment in her life.

"Dinner was great," Jack said. "But I think I'm going to head out to the lake and do a little fishing this evening. Probably won't catch as much as I would have in the early morning, but I'd like to try."

"Mind if I join you?" Travis asked.

Jack nodded. "I'd enjoy the company."

As everybody cleared their plates, Mia watched Travis and Jack walk out toward the lake, fishing poles in hand, and wondered just what the deal was. When had Travis been married? What exactly did she really know about his life?

TRAVIS LEANED back against the old wooden chair. He swore these were the same chairs that were there when he and Mia were teenagers. They used to love to sit out by the lake, although the dock wasn't built until years later. Some of his fondest memories of his childhood involved sitting there, casting his fishing line out into the still waters, surrounded by the blue colored mountains. There wasn't a more peaceful place on earth.

"So, your wife said you grew up around here?" he asked Jack. So far, Jack had been pretty tightlipped. He seemed like a nice enough guy, but very stiff and uncomfortable. Why anyone would want to go on vacation and then seem completely miserable was beyond him.

"Yeah, just down the road a ways. I haven't been back here in decades, though."

"I've been gone a while too. I grew up right here, fished in this lake a lot as a kid. But, after high school, I went off to chase my big dreams."

"Is that why Mia seems so upset at you?"

Jack was perceptive, he would give him that.

"Oh, so you picked up on that?" Travis said with a laugh.

"I have a wife who is often upset at me, so I recognize the signs," Jack said, a slight smile on his face. He was a tall man, towering above Travis by several inches. He was thin, lanky even, with salt and pepper hair and bright blue eyes. But he looked sad, like he was detached from his current reality.

"Mia was my high school sweetheart," Travis said. Jack cut him a look.

"Oh yes, I had one of those."

"So it wasn't Sylvia?"

"No. We've only been together for a little over twenty years. She's a good woman. I love her, but those high school sweethearts sure are hard to get out of your mind."

"Yes, they are. And trust me, Mia doesn't want me here in the slightest."

"Then why are you here?"

"Because I've spent so many years thinking about her that I couldn't handle it anymore. She was the one who got away."

"Why don't you tell her that?"

"Because Mia takes a little more... finessing... She's a hard nut to crack."

Jack chuckled. "In my experience, young man, you should never let a woman hear you say that you're finessing her. That will not go over well for you."

Travis laughed. "Then let's just keep it between us. I came here to see my parents, for one thing. But I'm staying here at the B&B because I want to try to talk to her. I want to make it up to her."

"What did you do?"

"We were really in love. I thought she'd be the woman I spent the rest of my life with. But she was really involved here at the B&B, helping her mother. I knew she wasn't ever going to leave this place, and I had all of these big dreams. I got a photography scholarship in New York City, and off I went, barely looking back. I broke her heart."

"We do stupid things when we're young. I know I made a lot of choices I regret in my life."

"Yeah, but what kind of loyalty did I show? I don't know why I took off and didn't even keep in touch. I think I just worried that she wouldn't want to speak to me. Then the years went by, I got married, my wife passed away. So much water under the bridge."

"But here you are now. Why?"

Travis reeled in his line and then threw it out again. "I guess because I'm getting older. I found myself thinking about her more and more as I got back out into the dating scene. I didn't even know if she was married or with someone, so I had my mom do a little bit of reconnaissance. When I found out she's still single, I decided to take a chance."

"So, you're here for love?"

"I guess you could say that."

"And how exactly are you going to accomplish this?"

Travis shrugged his shoulders. "Well, you see, I didn't get much beyond the romantic plan of getting her back. I have not a clue what I'm going to do."

Jack looked at him, a smile spreading across his face. "Maybe I can help you with that."

"Oh yeah?"

"Look, this place is pretty boring so far, so why don't you let me help you craft a plan. At least it'll be something to pass the time."

Travis nodded. "I can use all the help I can get."

MIA WAS surprised that Sylvia stayed behind when the men went fishing. Kate had a date with Cooper. They were apparently going bowling, something she never imagined that her new sister would do. She just didn't seem like the bowling type.

"I can finish cleaning up," Mia said, kind of hoping Sylvia would go upstairs. She liked to be left alone when doing housework. It gave her time to think, and it was a wonderful stress reliever.

"I don't mind. And who knows how long Jack will be out by that lake. He loves the water."

"Me too. I could sit out there all day," Mia said as she wiped down the breakfast bar countertop. It wasn't dirty, but she loved to keep a clean house. It was something her mother had taught her well.

"So, you mentioned your mother passed away. Mind if I ask what happened?"

"She died of cancer a few months ago." Mia hated saying the word cancer. It brought up so many memories that she wanted to forget. The visions of her mother going through that process in the last months of her life made her want to cry all over again.

"I'm so sorry to hear that. Losing a parent is incredibly hard. Were you close?"

Mia washed the sponge in the sink and then rung it out, setting it in the little holder that was suction cupped to the wall. "Very. It was just me and her most of the time growing up, and we ran this place together. I miss her every day."

"That story about you and your sister meeting is something else," Sylvia said.

Mia really hated small talk. And as much as she loved interacting with her guests, she preferred to keep her personal business out of it. Something about people knowing the intimate details of her life made her uncomfortable at times.

"Yes, it was an unexpected blessing. Momma would've been so excited to meet Kate. I'm just sorry that she never had the chance."

"Is that a picture of your mom?" Sylvia asked, pointing at a framed photo on the fireplace. She walked over and picked it up, staring at it closely.

Mia joined her in the living room. "That's her. That was taken about three years ago. We had such a good time running this place together. Sometimes I don't think I do nearly as good a job, but I strive to be like her every day."

Sylvia smiled. "She sounds like an incredible woman."

"No, she was an incredible human being. Everybody wanted to be like Charlene. All of our guests loved her. She had this amazing spirit that just permeated a room. There will never be anybody else like her." Her mother had been one of those people that made everyone around her feel good, even when she felt bad herself. Even in her illness, she smiled and greeted every guest until she could no longer stand on her feet anymore. She fought until the bitter end.

Sylvia put the picture back on the mantle. "It sounds like you were very lucky to have her."

Mia smiled. "I was."

"You don't know your father then?" Sylvia asked as she walked over and sat down on the sofa. Not wanting to be impolite, Mia followed suit and sat in the chair.

"No. I don't know anything about him, although recently I did get a connection on the DNA website. I've reached out, but he hasn't responded. I don't even think he knows that I exist."

"Oh. Did it tell you much about him?"

"No. No name or identifying information. I'm just sort of hoping that maybe he will reach out at some point. Honestly, I don't know what kind of person he is. Maybe I don't want to know him."

"I'm sure your mom had great taste," Sylvia said.

"Hopefully so. I don't know anything. She never would talk about him at all."

"Did you wonder why she wouldn't talk about him?"

"I have many times over the years. But I guess I might not ever get the answer."

"That would be sad, huh? Never knowing your father?"

"It would be, but I had such a wonderful mother that she more than made up for anything I think I would've missed. I prefer to leave it all in God's hands, you know?" In reality, she wanted to know her father more than anything. Just having another biological link would give her the stability she desperately needed after losing her mother.

Sylvia smiled graciously. "I'm sure things will work out like they're supposed to."

CHAPTER 5

*K*ate stood there, staring at the ten pins still standing, her ball disappearing into the dark depths of the gutter.

"I told you I suck at this game!" she said. Cooper laughed.

"But you look really cute throwing your ball."

She put her hands on her hips. "I don't think the people two lanes over thought it was really cute when my ball ended up in their lane!" She playfully stormed back over to the little plastic chair and sat down.

"You have to keep them on their toes," Cooper said, picking up his ball and holding it up in the air to line it up with the pins. His arm came back and then tossed the ball forward. Kate watched as it went straight down the middle and knocked down all ten pins, giving him yet another strike.

This was embarrassing. She prided herself on being good at things, but bowling definitely wasn't one of them.

"And that's the game," she said, praying to God that he didn't want to play again. They had already played three games, and she was getting tired of losing.

"I'm going to assume that you don't want to play again?" Cooper asked, with a wink. She hated that he was so cute. Right now she wanted to slug him, her competitive spirit bubbling just under the surface.

"I think I've had enough for tonight," she said, as she leaned over and took off the God awful clown shoes she had been forced to wear. Several different shades of brown accented by one patch of orange. They were the ugliest things she'd seen in a while.

He sat down across from her and started taking off his shoes. "You know, they have an arcade here."

Kate laughed. "Are you saying you want to spend the rest of the evening playing Pac-Man or something?"

"I'm pretty sure Pac-Man isn't really all the rage these days. Most of the kids in here wouldn't even know what that was."

She nodded. "You're probably right. Although, I did see an air hockey table."

He looked at her carefully. "And you think you can beat me at air hockey?"

"No. I *know* I can beat you at air hockey."

Cooper chuckled. "That sounds like a challenge to me."

"Are you up for it?"

He stared at her for a long moment. "If we're going to have an actual challenge, don't you think we should have a prize?"

"Okay. What kind of prize?"

"Well, if I win, you have to cook me dinner at the B&B and have a candlelight meal in the gazebo."

"And if I win?"

"Well, what do you want?"

"Hmmm… Let me think… If I win, you have to strip down to your boxer shorts and jump in that freezing cold lake."

Cooper's eyes widened. "Wow. That's really mean!"

"Then I guess you better win," Kate said, hitting his leg with her bowling shoes before trotting off to return them.

MIA WAS KIND OF ENJOYING HAVING the house to herself for a little while. Her sister and Cooper were still on their date, and Sylvia and Jack had decided to go listen to some music at a place in town. She got the feeling that there was some conflict between the two of them, but she couldn't quite put a finger on it.

So far, she hadn't gotten to know much about Jack. He was kind of standoffish, obviously not super happy to be there. She didn't know why, but it wasn't her job to know. She was just the owner of a bed-and-break-fast, and she couldn't get too involved in other people's affairs.

She walked upstairs and slowly opened the door to her mother's office. It was difficult going through everything, and sometimes she enjoyed having Kate there to help her. Other times, she just needed a moment to herself, just a minute to reflect on how much she truly missed her mother. Her smile. Her life. Her incredible sense of graciousness and southern hospitality. But mostly the way that she made Mia feel like everything was going to be okay, no matter what the world threw at her.

Over the last few days, she had managed to clean the top of her mother's desk as well as the file cabinet. Most of it wasn't anything personal, just a lot of old files and tax paperwork. She had decided she would put most of them in the safe, just in case their accountant ever needed any of it.

Tonight, she was going to start tackling the closet. It was the place she was most likely to find something more personal of her mother's, and she wasn't sure whether to be excited or nervous.

Since finding her raincoat in the closet the other day, she hadn't opened it again. She knew there was a lot more behind that door that she needed to go through, things that her mother had never shown her in all her years of life.

She reached onto the shelf and pulled off a worn cardboard box. Charlene's name was written on the side of it. It was probably things that she took with her when she moved out of her own mother's house.

She set the box on the desk and opened it up. A plume of dust assaulted her nose as she let out a sneeze and wiped at the dust in air with her hand.

Most of what she found were pictures of Charlene when she was little. Standing at preschool, holding up a paper turkey she'd made. Standing in front of the Christmas tree. Standing with her mother in what was

probably her Easter dress. All of the requisite pictures
one would expect. There were also pictures of Mia
when she was little, some that she had never seen
before. Her mother holding her as a newborn. Her
mother rocking her in her grandmother's old rocking
chair. Mia smiled when she saw those younger
versions of her mother. It made her seem more alive
again.

When she finished going through the box, she
sealed it up and placed it back on the shelf. One day,
she would get some nice photo albums to display all of
the pictures. For now, she just didn't have the time to
give it the energy that it needed.

Just as she was about to shut the closet door, she
saw a floral box in the back corner. She'd never seen
this box before, and it didn't have anything written on
it. It wasn't overly big, but it was a beautiful, old box.

She stood up on her tiptoes, trying to reach it as
best she could, but to no avail. Being short definitely
had its drawbacks, and this was one of the moments.

She decided that it was futile; there was no way she
was going to be able to reach that box without some
help. Remembering that there was a footstool in
Travis's room, she decided to go swipe it while he was
gone. She hadn't seen him since he went fishing with
Jack earlier in the evening, so she had to assume that he
had gone to visit his parents.

She poked her head out the door and saw that
Travis's door was closed. She walked over and tapped
on it lightly, nobody answering. She knocked a little
harder, but again no answer. After waiting a few extra

moments, she turned the handle and pushed the door open. Thankfully, his room was dark. She flipped on the light and walked over to pick up the stool. Just as she picked it up and headed back out into the hallway, the bathroom door opened.

In that moment, she was very lucky not to have broken her toe by dropping the stool.

Time stood still as she found herself staring face-to-face with Travis wearing nothing but a fluffy white towel. His hair was wet, his body glistening, his muscles better than they had been in high school. Where did he get such a good tan at this time of the year? And how strong was that towel? Was it going to fall down at any moment? Was there a chance she might just rip it right off and snatch it away?

"Travis!"

"Mia?"

"What are you doing here? I didn't even know you were home."

"I was taking a shower…" he said, pointing at the bathroom behind him.

"Why didn't I hear the water?" Realizing the washing machine was also running downstairs, she hadn't put two and two together when she heard the water running through the pipes earlier.

"I'm sorry, Mia. I didn't know there were rules against me taking a shower."

She could feel her face turning redder and redder. This was the part of having an Irish heritage that she hated. "And you were just gonna walk out here in the hallway wearing nothing but a towel?"

"My room is two feet away. I thought I would be safe," he said with a wink.

"Next time, wear a bathrobe or something," she said, quickly turning and heading back toward the office. She slammed the door behind her, put the stool on the floor in front of the closet and took in a deep breath.

She couldn't believe what she just saw. Why was he even more handsome in his thirties than he was when he was sixteen years old? Everything had filled out. Even those little crows' feet around his eyes were handsome. He looked like he could be one of those anchormen on TV.

She had never expected to feel this way about anyone again, and certainly not Travis Norton. Something about him just got under her skin. Memories flooded back every time she looked at him, and so did regrets.

Trying to push away the past, she stepped up onto the stool to reach for the box again. Still, her arms were too short. Why was this dang closet so deep? For a moment, she considered just climbing onto the top shelf, but with her luck it would probably come crashing down and she'd split her head open. And then Travis would have to use that white towel to stop the bleeding and...

"Do you need some help?" he said from the doorway. She needed to get her hearing checked. First she hadn't heard the shower and now she hadn't heard him open the door.

"You're trespassing." She knew it was a stupid statement, but it was all she could think of at the time.

"I don't think so. I'm paying to stay here." He smiled that lazy smile that made her want to kick him in the teeth. Or maybe kiss him. She couldn't tell which one.

"What do you want?"

"I'd like to help you," he said. Thankfully, now he was wearing a pair of gray gym shorts and a lighter gray T-shirt. His hair was still wet, although combed. There was a little piece of it that hung in his face, but it didn't look messy. It looked sexy, and that made her mad.

"No, I've got it."

She turned to ignore him, and tried reaching up again. This time, she hadn't paid close enough attention to where her feet were positioned on the stool. Her tiptoes were on the edge and, before she knew it, the stool was tipping over toward the closet, about to send her into a wonderful face plant against the wooden shelf.

Before that could happen, somehow within a split second, she felt his strong arms around her waist, pulling her backward. She was holding onto the shelf so tightly that the force pulled it out of the wall with them. Travis fell to the floor on his back, and Mia landed on top of him on her back while a whole host of boxes fell on top of them both. Of course, none of them were the floral box. She could see it still sitting on its little shelf in the back corner, dang it.

Then, there was silence. Had he been knocked out? Did she need to call the ambulance? They both just laid there, neither of them moving, his arms still firmly around her waist. She saw his fingers move, and at least she knew he was still alive.

"Are you okay?" she asked.

"I think so. I might have a headache."

She did her best to push off the boxes and pictures that had landed on top of her and scooted herself around to face him. This was bad news. She was currently laying on top of Travis Norton, now face-to-face.

"Are you all right?" he asked her. Oh Lord. Looking into his eyes was like going home again. She had to get up, and fast.

She scooted off of him and onto the floor next to him.

"I'm fine. I don't know why you grabbed me. I pulled the darn shelf out of the wall!"

"I'll help you fix it."

He slowly sat up, rubbing the back of his head. "And I'll have you know, if I hadn't grabbed you, you were going to hit that pretty little face of yours right on the wood."

He said she had a pretty face. *Don't get distracted. Don't get distracted.*

"I don't need you to fix it. I can fix it. Or I'll get Cooper to do it."

"Cooper? Cooper from high school?"

"The very same one."

"Don't tell me you're dating Cooper!"

"What if I'm married to him?" she said, unsure of why she was poking and prodding him like this.

"You're married to Cooper?"

Mia chuckled loudly. "Of course I'm not married to Cooper. But he is dating my sister. "

"After how he treated you in high school? I'm surprised you let that idiot anywhere around you."

She sighed. "At first, I didn't. But he and my sister are falling for each other, and he apologized. In fact, he built my deck and my gazebo out back. For free."

"So your love can be purchased?"

"Talk to me after you build me a gazebo," she said, sarcastically. She stood up and started gathering things back into the boxes.

She could've asked him to get the floral box for her, but she didn't want to give him the satisfaction. Right now, she just wanted to get him out of her mother's office.

"Look, I'm sorry I startled you in the hallway. And I'm sorry I saved you from hitting your face, although I'm not sure why I should be sorry for that. But I'm not sorry I can't stand Cooper."

She turned around, one hand on her hip. "Well, then it's a good thing you're only here temporarily, isn't it? After all, I'm sure you have places to go and people to see. No need to worry about my life or what's going on with me once you've left. Now, if you'll excuse me, I have some work to do." She pointed at all the things on the floor.

Travis leaned down to pick something up. "Let me help you…"

"No! Just go, Travis. Please."

He stood up, slowly, and looked at her. There was a hurt on his face she hadn't expected.

"Okay. I'll go. But I hope one day you'll give me a chance to explain some things to you. I think there are a lot of things between us that need to be said."

He walked toward the door and just as he was shutting it, looked back at her one more time, his mouth moving to speak. She spoke before he could.

"Breakfast is at seven AM. Pancakes and bacon tomorrow."

He nodded and shut the door behind him.

EVIE REACHED across the table to grab the syrup. Kate lightly swatted her hand.

"Where are your manners? You don't reach across my plate!"

Evie rolled her eyes like the teenager she was. "Sorry, your highness. Can I have the syrup, if you please?" she said with a fake British accent.

Kate shook her head and passed the syrup to her daughter. Sometimes she didn't know where that child got her sassy attitude. She didn't remember being that way as a teenager. Her parents would've had her head on a platter if she'd talked back to them.

"Cut her some slack," Mia said, smiling. "After all, she starts school on Monday. New school, new friends, new place. How are you feeling about it?"

She shrugged her shoulders. "I mean, it's just school. Nothing important."

Kate slapped her hand on the table lightly. "Young lady, you better take it seriously. If you don't, there's absolutely nothing else I can do but homeschool you. Is that what you want?"

Evie laughed. "That is absolutely not what I want. I tried to get you to help me with my math last year, and I literally saw your eyes start to tear up."

Kate looked at Mia. "Math is hard. Have you seen the way they teach them nowadays?"

Mia giggled. "I guess it's one of the perks of not having children yet. No math homework to worry about," she said, carrying her plate over to the sink.

The first part of breakfast had been interacting with the guests, but now that everybody had gone on with their day, the three of them were able to sit down for breakfast alone.

"So, what's your plan for this fine Friday afternoon?" Mia asked as she rinsed off her plate.

"Well, Cooper wants to take me on a hike. And then I think we're getting dinner in town later."

"What about you Evie? Any big plans?"

"Oh yes. First I'm going to watch TV, then I'm going to stare at my phone and then I'm going to go to sleep." She stood up and walked over to put her plate in the sink. Mia pointed at it, reminding her to wash it off and put it in the dishwasher.

"Don't worry, Evie. I'm sure you're going to meet lots of new friends next week. You'll have a full social calendar before you know it," Mia said, ever the optimist.

"I don't care. I've never been a person who needed a lot of friends."

It made Kate sad to hear her say something like

that. She absolutely needed friends, but she had put up such a wall over the years after being abandoned by her father that she wanted everyone to think she didn't need anyone.

"Hey, sweetie, you're more than welcome to come hiking with me and Cooper. He wouldn't mind at all," Kate said.

She shook her head. "No thanks. Honestly, I'm looking forward to spending the night binge watching a show. I'll probably be asleep before you get home."

"Be asleep? That early?"

"I have to get ready for school, don't I? I'm going to organize my backpack, check in on social media and then go to sleep early. "

"But you have the whole weekend. Why would you go to sleep early tonight?" Kate asked.

"Because I'll probably be tired after binge watching TV. You know how I am. My eyes get exhausted and I'm out like a light."

"Plus, she probably needs to start going to bed early to get her body ready to wake up on Monday morning," Mia said, winking at her.

Kate guessed that made some sense, although her daughter had never offered to go to bed early. Maybe she was finally maturing a bit.

"Well, I'll bring you some dessert anyway. At least you can have it tomorrow after lunch. Cooper said the restaurant has amazing blueberry cheesecake."

"That sounds good. I'm going to go sit in my tree and do some journaling for a while," Evie said, as she walked toward the front door. She had her backpack slung over her shoulder.

"Okay. Just don't go far and don't go near that creek…" Kate called.

Evie turned around. "I know, Mom. I'm not going to do anything stupid."

As she walked out the door, Kate struggled to believe her. She worried that when she met new friends at the high school, she'd find her self in trouble all over again. But she had to let go and give her some room to make a new life. How she did in school would greatly affect whether they would ever go back to Rhode Island or finally decide to make their permanent home in Carter's Hollow.

CHAPTER 6

*M*ia stood in the kitchen, doing what she did best - cooking. She was working on making a batch of her mother's peach cobbler, somewhat for the guests but also to put into the freezer and reheat at a future date. It was a time intensive process to get it right, so she hoped that the frozen versions would be as palatable as the fresh.

Everybody had gone out for the day, Kate and Cooper were on their hike, Evie was in her tree somewhere and Sylvia and Jack had driven a couple of towns over to visit the home where he'd grown up.

Mia still didn't know much about him or his wife, and she wasn't sure they would ever come back in the future. Repeat guests were an important part of the B&B, and she valued them greatly. People became like family over the years, and it made her feel less alone now that her mother was gone.

Still, this couple seemed to have secrets, from the outside world and maybe even from each other. She didn't quite understand what was going on between them. Maybe they were trying to save their marriage in some kind of a last ditch effort. Maybe they were just unhappy. Maybe Jack was cheating on Sylvia or Sylvia was living a secret life.

Or maybe she just read too many mystery novels.

Still, she enjoyed having the place to herself most afternoons. It gave her time to think and clear her head. Of course, she didn't have a whole lot to think about lately other than the fact that she had seen Travis with his shirt off and a towel wrapped around his waist. Or the fact that he had put those very strong arms around her and broken her fall. Or the fact that he had told her she had a pretty face, something she hadn't heard from a man in a very long time.

She would be very glad when he left. Because of her love of his parents, she kept allowing him to stay there, but she wasn't sure how much longer she could do it. She only had a certain amount of strength.

She wrapped the last peach cobbler and put it into the freezer while popping the other one into the oven. The smell immediately started to permeate the room as it heated up. Every time she smelled it, she thought of her mother.

There were so many memories of her standing in the kitchen with her momma, mixing the dough and pouring the peaches out of the canning jar. For a long time, her mother made it with fresh peaches from the area. But then she started canning her own, and those were just as good. In fact, they often tasted a lot sweeter.

Thankfully, she still had a lot of those canned peaches in her pantry, but one day soon she would start to can her own just like her mother did. She would start to take over and do the things her momma taught her, although she wasn't sure if she'd ever measure up.

Many times, she thought about the fact that she didn't have a daughter of her own. She didn't have any kids at all, and that made her sad. If there was one thing that Mia had always wanted, it was to be a mother. And now, in her thirties, it wasn't looking very likely. She wanted someone to share these things with, someone to pass those family stories and recipes on to one day. Maybe it would just be something she could give to her niece, Evie. But it wasn't the same.

"I remember that smell." She turned around to see Travis standing there, his hands in his jean pockets. How he managed to look so casual and so much like a catalog model at the same time was beyond her. His hair was slightly tousled and a little bit wet, his button up shirt untucked on one side, just messy enough to make him look handsome.

"Oh. I didn't know you were here."

"I just came in. Did a little fishing this morning."

She smiled slightly. "I don't remember you doing this much fishing when we were growing up."

He walked closer and sat at one of the barstools at the breakfast bar. "You don't realize the things that you miss about home until you come back. Like that peach cobbler you have in the oven."

"Yes, if I ever leave this place, that peach cobbler will go with me everywhere."

"Do you think you'll ever leave?"

That question took her back. He had asked her the same question so many years ago before he finally left. Her answer had always been no, and it still was. Just the fact that he was asking it again pushed her back into reality with a violent shove.

"No. I would never give up my mother's legacy here. That hasn't changed, Travis."

He nodded. "I figured as much. This place is in your blood, Mia. I can't imagine you being anywhere else."

"Listen, this isn't going to be done for a while. But I'll be glad to save you some for dinner tonight if you'd like." She just wanted to get out of there. She took off her apron, wiping her hands on it before she put it back on the hook on the wall.

"Actually, I was going to ask you something."

"And what's that?"

"Well, do you mind if I use the old canoe out there?"

"The big one? Of course not. It hasn't been used in a while, so you might want to check it for any damage."

"Right… Well… I was hoping you might go with me."

"Go with you? To check for damage? I'm pretty sure you can do that yourself, Travis."

"No," he said, smiling. "I wanted to know if you'd go out on the lake with me for a little while. I mean, the peach cobbler has to cook so is there anything else you have to do right now?"

Her stomach churned, butterflies doing somersaults

like they were Olympic athletes. "Travis, I don't think that's a very good idea."

"You can just set a timer. I promise you I'll get you back so it doesn't burn."

She stared at him. "I'm not worried about it burning."

He paused for a moment and nodded. "Oh. You just don't want to go with me?"

"Like I said, I don't think it's a very good idea. I mean, I'm letting you stay here but nothing has really changed…"

"Mia, I'm not asking you to elope or something. I was just wondering if you might keep me company in the canoe for a little bit. For old time's sake?"

As teenagers, they were often out on the lake in one of the canoes. Some of her fondest moments with Travis were spent on the still waters underneath the beautiful mountain views. Often, they would stay out there for hours, laughing, drinking Coca-Cola straight out of the glass bottles and eating ham and cheese sandwiches that her mother had made them. Such simple times, yet such stirring memories in her soul.

"I don't know…" She knew she should just say no. No was the right answer. Everything in her brain was screaming no over and over again. She could hear Raven's voice echoing in her head. "Okay, I guess so."

Travis looked surprised, but he grinned. "Really? Great. Let's go then!" She walked toward him, and he opened the front door, letting her out first like the Southern gentleman that he had always been.

As they headed toward the water, Mia second-guessed herself a thousand times, but she just couldn't seem to make her feet stop. For some reason, she just needed to relive some moments with Travis Norton on that lake. Maybe it would give her closure, or maybe it would be the worst decision of her life.

KATE DIDN'T KNOW why she had allowed Cooper to talk her into going on a hike. She wasn't the hiking type. She much preferred nice hotels, manicures and pedicures. But she found herself standing in the middle of the woods, crunchy leaves at her feet, and it wasn't so bad. It was hot and humid, but not so bad.

And the company was even better. All she could think about every time she went somewhere with Cooper was when was he going to make his move? When was he finally going to kiss her? And why wasn't she making the move herself?

Dating was difficult. She hadn't done it in a long time, and it hadn't gotten any easier. What were the rules, anyway? Why couldn't she just grab him, plant a big wet kiss on his lips and get it over with?

"You seem lost in thought," Cooper said, as they stopped to take a breather and a water break.

"No. Just enjoying the scenery and the company."

He laughed. "You know, you wouldn't have said that about me a few weeks ago. You weren't my biggest fan when we first met."

"Well, let's be real. You were kind of a jerk."

"Agreed. Sometimes my wonderful personality comes off a little bit abrasive. I get that."

"And I don't think you liked me very much either," Kate said, taking a long drink of her water.

"You're wrong about that. I knew from the first time I met you that I liked you."

"Oh yeah? And why is that?"

"I think it was because you're so different than the other women around here. I love southern women, don't get me wrong. But there was an edge about you, and I felt like you could take me. I guess that's why I was testing you."

"Oh, you were testing me, were you?" she said, poking him in the chest.

"Maybe a little."

"Well, so far I think you passed the test pretty well. But if you get me lost in these woods, I'm going to have to take off quite a few points."

He chuckled. "Don't you worry, ma'am. I've never gotten lost in these woods. I know my way around them like the back of my hand. And that's why I wanted to bring you to this place."

She looked around. They were in a completely nondescript area of the woods, the trail barely visible below their feet. "I'm feeling kind of lost right now, Cooper. No offense, but this place isn't all that special."

"You haven't seen anything yet. Come on," he said, reaching out his hand. She loved when he held her hand. His was big and firm and a little bit rough. The few men she had dated in Rhode Island didn't have

hands like that. Brandon's hands had been more femi-
nine than hers, in fact.

They walked down a slight hill, and then took a
turn down another trail. It felt like he was getting them
more and more lost, and everything looked the same to
her. Then she started hearing the sound of water.

"Are you ready for this?" he asked.

"I don't know. Am I?" she responded, laughing.

He helped her down a much steeper area and then
she saw it. There was a huge rock waterfall, but it was
smooth. It looked like God had made a water slide
down the edge of a mountain that landed in a beautiful
pool below. She'd never seen anything like it. It seemed
so magical out in the middle of nowhere, and nobody
was there.

"Wow! What is this?"

"This is a natural water slide. When we were kids,
we would all come here on Sundays after church and
spend hours sliding down this rock into the pool
below. The water is pretty cold, no matter what time of
year."

"Are we going to get in?" she asked, incredulously.

"Of course we are! Why would I bring you here and
not get in?"

It dawned on her that he'd told her to wear clothing
that she didn't mind getting a little messed up. So she
wore some khaki shorts, an old navy blue T-shirt and
her most comfortable sneakers. Of course, she hadn't
realized he wanted her to careen down a mountainside
into a pool of unknown water. What was it with mountain people?

"You have to be a crazy person to think that I'm going to slide down the side of a rock. Do I look like I'm a daredevil?"

Cooper smiled. "Don't worry. I've done this a million times, and I've only seen a few people get hurt."

She stared at him, her mouth hanging open. "Is that supposed to make me feel better?"

He walked forward and put his hands on her upper arms. Maybe this was the moment…

"I would never, ever let anything bad happen to you, Kate. Okay?"

For some reason, that made her feel better, even though she knew it was very likely she was going to bonk her head on the rock and forget who she was for the rest of her life.

"Fine. But if I get hurt, you have to make sure that Evie gets a big settlement from whoever owns this property."

He laughed. "Done."

She followed him to the top of the rock. Surprisingly, nobody was there, but it was probably because it was the last weekend before school and parents were keeping their kids home to get ready for the year ahead.

She was glad to have the place to themselves. It was magical and romantic, and floating in a pool of water with Cooper didn't seem like such a bad idea.

In her late thirties, she never expected to be falling for somebody all over again. She hoped he felt the same way, but they hadn't had very many deep conversations about it. Dating in her thirties was certainly different than dating in her early twenties. Back then, it had been with an eye toward marriage and building a family. That certainly hadn't worked out like she had planned.

"Okay, you're gonna wanna put your phone and anything else you don't want to get wet over here on the rock. Nobody's out here, so we don't have to worry about anything getting stolen."

She did as he said, taking her phone and her keys out of her pocket and placing it on a big smooth rock under an overhang. She also took off her shoes and pulled her hair up into a messy bun on top of her head.

"I like that," he said, with a slight smile. Even though it was hot, she felt some cool shivers run up her spine.

"It's my messy librarian look." She turned back and forth like she was posing for a camera.

"I used to have a huge crush on our school librarian when I was in elementary school. Mrs. Dalrymple. She wore these long, plaid wool skirts, support hose and chunky little heels that had these big gold medallions on them. And, most importantly, she smelled like pancakes."

Kate let out a loud laugh that echoed around the canyon. "That's a visual I didn't need."

"She was hot. I mean she was like sixty, but anybody who smells like pancakes is good in my book."

She couldn't get over how much she enjoyed spending time with him. He made her laugh. That was something that Brandon had never really been able to do. For a long time, Brandon had made her feel safe, but he never had a funny bone.

"Are you ready?" She wasn't, but she nodded her head anyway. They stood at the top of the water, and he grabbed her hand once again. "Just hold on to me."

Seconds later, they leaned forward slightly, sat down on their butts and went flying down the rock. It wasn't that long, but it was a wild ride. She struggled to hold onto his hand, before her fingertips finally slipped away as they hit the big pool.

To her surprise, it wasn't super deep. When she went under the water, she immediately felt the bottom, so she assumed it was probably only seven or eight feet deep.

When she came up for air, she saw Cooper a few feet from her, bobbing above the surface, a big grin on his face.

"What'd you think?" he called over to her, the sound of the water behind them making it a little harder to hear.

"That was amazing!" she called back. It really had been. Kate had never been a risk taker. The one time she had ridden a roller coaster when she was a teenager, she'd thrown up on her friend and spent the rest of the day with vertigo. Brandon had tried to talk her into skydiving, and that was a big fat no. One of her friends wanted her to go parasailing on vacation at the beach, and she had refused that too.

Cooper swam over to her. "Wasn't that cool? Gosh, it's been so long since I did that, but it really brought back old memories."

"I bet. Can we do it again?" Kate asked, a sly smile on her face.

Cooper stared at her for a long moment. "Really?"

"Yeah. I've never done anything so exhilarating in my life!"

"What about this?"

Without warning, she felt his hands pull her closer, and then she felt his lips on hers. Warm and wet and welcoming. And then she realized that the most exhilarating thing that had ever happened to her was what was happening right now.

CHAPTER 7

*M*ia was second-guessing everything about her life right now. As they pushed away from the dock, she suddenly felt very trapped. Being alone with Travis had never been a good thing for her. He had a way about him, one of those personalities that everybody wanted to be around.

Back in high school, all of the girls swooned over Travis. He was an old soul, as her mother would say. He wrote poetry, took photographs and even dabbled in painting. Yet he was also a star on the baseball team and had even wrestled for a year, almost making state champion.

He was one of the most well-rounded people she'd ever met in her life, which was one of the reasons that it hurt so much when he left. She'd always felt like he was too good for her, and when he drove away that day, it was just further confirmed in her mind.

At first, they were both quiet, the tension between them thick enough to cut with a knife. Mia thought for a moment about her swimming skills and whether she could just "accidentally" topple over the side of the canoe and make her way back to the dock. Of course, then she'd look like a dirty, drowned rat by the time she got back to the B&B.

"I'm glad you agreed to come with me," Travis finally said.

Travis stopped rowing and put the oar in its holder. The lake was so still and beautiful, like a piece of glass. There was no sound, other than the occasional squawking bird off in the distance. The blue tinge of the mountains above them cast a perfect reflection against the stillness of the water. It was beautiful, but she was more uncomfortable than she had been in a while.

"Well, I knew you weren't going to let it go, so I thought it best to just humor you."

He chuckled under his breath. "Well, whatever the reason, I'm just glad you're here with me."

She couldn't take it anymore. "Travis, why are you doing this? I agreed to let you stay here because of your father, but I don't understand all of this." She waved her hand in the air, gesturing about everything that had been going on between them since he showed up. The tension. The uncomfortable moments. The towel.

"What do you mean?"

"You could've just come here and stayed out of my way. Just like any other guest. I don't go out on canoes with the other guests."

"Then why are you here with me right now?"

"That's a good question. Honestly, I have no idea."

"Look, I knew I needed to get you away from the B&B for a few minutes so we could talk."

"Talk about what?"

"The past."

She shook her head and put up her hands. "No. I don't have any need to talk about the past."

"You know, you've always been like this. Sometimes you can be really insufferable."

She stared at him, her mouth hanging open and her eyes wide. "Excuse me? I'm insufferable?"

"You might be a tiny little person, but you're as stubborn as a mule."

"Oh yeah? Well at least I don't leave people behind and take off to New York City and forget they ever existed!" she said, screaming so loudly that it echoed around the canyon. She slapped her hand over her mouth, trying to keep any more words from flying out that she wasn't expecting.

Travis looked at her for a very long moment and then looked down. "You're right."

"What?"

"I want to apologize, Mia. I did so many things wrong that it's hard to even add them all up."

"I'm listening," she said, softly, just wanting to know how this was going to play out.

He took in a deep breath, blew it out and then rubbed his hands over the tops of his legs, something he had always done when he was nervous. "I always thought that I wouldn't be living my full life if I stayed here in this place. I love Carter's Hollow, but at that age I thought you were supposed to leave high school and go take on the world. And when I got that opportunity, it went to my head. I felt like it was my only option of ever making something out of myself."

"We had dated for over two years, Travis. And you drove away like I didn't even matter." Her eyes started to well with tears, so she turned her head and blinked quickly, trying to will them away. Her logical mind told her that it was ridiculous to be this upset over something that happened so many years ago.

"I know that's how it must've felt. But I knew you would never leave this place because of your mother. You made it very clear you had to stay here and help her after Bobby died. So, I thought if I went and made something of myself, you might be willing to take a chance to come be with me."

"Okay, so even if that's true, why didn't you ever send me a letter? Call me on the phone? I don't know, send a Telegram or a pigeon with a note?"

He shrugged his shoulders. "I don't know. At first, I was so focused on what I was doing at school that I just kept my head down. I wanted to have some real success to write home about. I didn't want to fail right out of the gate and have to crawl back home with my tail between my legs. Plus, I knew that if I talked to you, I would miss you so much that I would just turn around and come right back home anyway."

"Do you know how much that hurt? It was like a dagger to my heart."

He looked at her, his face soft, regret painted in every little line that was starting to form. "I'm sorry. I really am."

"Then you got married?"

He sighed. "I met Nanette in my third year of college. By that point, I hadn't even come home to visit. I knew you hated me. I felt like I had to start over. So, we met through a mutual friend, she was smart and nice and loved me, so we got married about a year and a half later. We were only married for two years before she got diagnosed."

"I'm so sorry. I have no right to even talk about your marriage."

"Look, I want you to know everything about my life. You can ask me any question you want. I know things may never be the same between us again, but even if we had some kind of friendship, that would mean the world to me."

"What have you been doing in your career?" she asked, hoping that question would divert him away from asking her to be his friend.

"Well, that's the most embarrassing part of this whole thing."

"Why?"

"You know how much I loved taking photos, especially of the nature around here. I loved it. And I thought that's what I'd end up doing for my job, maybe being a travel photographer or something like that. But for more than a decade, I've been a fast food photographer."

"What is that? A fast food photographer?"

He laughed under his breath. "You know how when you go to the drive through at those fast food places and they have those delectable photos of hamburgers and parfait cups on the board where you order?"

"Yes…"

"Well, I'm the guy who takes those pictures. Pretty impressive, huh?" He rolled his eyes and shook his head.

That made her feel heartsick. She didn't want anything bad to happen to Travis, and all this time she thought he was jet setting around the globe, pursuing his love of photography. Instead he'd been stuck somewhere taking pictures of hamburgers and chicken sandwiches, widowed and not pursuing his dreams at all.

"I never expected that."

"Neither did I. But sometimes we make choices that put us on a path we don't even recognize. And that's where I've been all these years. I still live in New York, and every day I go into my office and make crappy food look really good."

"Yeah, the food never looks anything like those pictures," Mia said, laughing.

"You wouldn't believe the tricks we employ to make you want to eat it," he said, with a wink. "So, in the end, I became the exact person I didn't want to be, Mia. I thought you were crazy for staying here, getting stuck in Carter's Hollow. The fact is, I'm the one who's been stuck all these years."

She didn't know what to say. "I better get back before the peach cobbler burns."

He nodded, picked up the oar and started rowing

toward the dock again. "I'm glad we got a chance to talk, Mia. I hope we can do it again sometime soon."

"Maybe," she said. Right now, she had no idea how to feel.

EVIE PULLED BACK her covers and took every pillow she had in her room plus a couple from the guest rooms that were unoccupied, and put them underneath. Pulling the cover up, she tucked it under the pillows like a burrito to make it look like someone was sleeping in the bed.

It was just getting dark, so she would have to wait a little while longer before she could make her move.

Thankfully, her mother and Cooper were out on a date after spending the day hiking. She liked Cooper, but it was unusual for her to see her mother spending so much time with someone. It'd always just been the two of them, and there was a small part of her that was starting to feel a little jealous. The last thing she wanted to do was lose another parent like her dad had lost interest in her so long ago.

Her Aunt Mia was downstairs cleaning up after dinner, and Travis had gone to see his parents. The other couple, the old people, were probably in their room for the night after eating dinner with Mia downstairs.

The meal had been a little awkward and uncomfort-able. Mia tried to be engaging, but it was obvious something had happened between her and Travis earlier in the day because the conversation was kind of strained. The older couple didn't really talk much at all, and Evie didn't know why they were even on this vacation.

Right now, all she needed to worry about was safely getting out of the house and over to the party. Dustin had given her directions on how to get there, but he said he would meet her at the tree just so she didn't get lost in the dark woods. It wasn't overly far, maybe a mile and a half, but she knew her mother would've told her no if she had asked.

Making it look like she was asleep in her bed was the only way she knew how to get out of the house and be able to have fun without worrying. She would sneak back in before morning, and nobody would be the wiser.

She peeked out her window to make sure the coast was clear and quietly opened it. Thankfully, her window went out onto a flat part of the roof. There was a large tree nearby that she could shimmy down, her climbing skills having gotten better since moving out into the country.

Before she knew it, she had slid down the tree, only one little scrape on her inner thigh, and landed on the ground, her backpack slung over her shoulder.

She looked around again just to make sure nobody could see her and then scurried up the driveway, hoping like heck that her mother and Cooper didn't come home right at that moment and see her.

Thankfully, nobody was coming and she was able to

get to the tree. Dustin was standing there, leaning against it, waiting for her.

"What took you so long? The party has been going on for an hour."

"Look, it was all I could do to get out of there. Dinner went on and on."

"Did you bring your own burger?"

"I thought you were joking about that."

He shook his head and laughed. "We are simple people here, and we like burgers. Don't worry. I brought one for you."

"Good. Let's get out of here before we get caught!"

She followed him through the dark woods, down one trail and then another. He seemed to know them like the back of his hand, and that was a good thing because she had gotten lost in them already more than once.

Finally, off in the distance she could see a huge bonfire. Smoke was billowing out of the top of it into the dark night sky. People were laughing and talking. She saw a game of corn hole over on one side and then a group of giggling high school girls on the other. She would steer clear of them. Those just weren't her type of people.

Of course, she saw plenty of people drinking cans of beer. She wasn't about to try to go home with alcohol on her breath. Her mother would never let her out of the house again.

Behind the area was a huge water tower with Carter's Hollow painted on the side of it. She had seen it when they first drove into town.

"Let me introduce you to some people," Dustin said, taking her around to several of his friends, mostly guys. They all seemed nice enough, much more down to earth than the type of people she knew at her high school back in Rhode Island.

For the next couple of hours, they all sat back and relaxed, watching the fire and eventually cooking the burgers. People were telling her stories of crazy things Dustin had done over the years, like tipping cows and toilet papering the school principal's house. Most of the kids had known each other since elementary school, and she wished she had those kinds of relationships with friends her age. But she really didn't.

"So you're from up north?" One guy, nicknamed Bubba, asked her. At least she hoped that was only a nickname. He was wearing a pair of jeans stained with Georgia red clay, a pair of work boots and a flannel shirt. His hat, which was, of course, turned backward, had dirt on it too. She wondered what he'd been doing all day.

"Yeah. Rhode Island."

"Never been there before. I ain't been north of Tennessee!"

"Don't mind Bubba. He's not exactly a world traveler," Dustin said under his breath.

"Why are you so dirty?" she asked Bubba. Everybody laughed.

"I work on my daddy's farm. Had to catch a pig today. He didn't want to be caught." Again, everybody laughed. Evie had to admit that they were easy to get along with, even some of the girls. She didn't feel judged. They seemed genuinely interested in her, Which was not something she was used to.

"Why do y'all meet here at the water tower?"

"Should we tell her?" Bubba said. The crowd erupted in a loud roar.

"Tell me what?"

"Every year, right before school starts back, we climb up to the top of that water tower. We paint our school's mascot and tag it."

"Tag it?"

"You know, spray paint. Like graffiti," Bubba said, throwing up his hands.

"Oh, I'm not doing that. I'm terrified of heights."

"You gotta do it. It's a tradition!" Bubba insisted.

"You don't have to go if you don't want to," Dustin said quietly.

If there was one thing Evie couldn't tolerate, it was people thinking she was a coward. And right now, every person was looking at her. "So do you all climb up there?"

"No. Only the brave among us," Bubba said. "Usually me, Dustin and the rest of these idiots right here."

A bunch of the guys lifted their cans of soda or beer in the air. None of the girls said a peep. This was her chance to stand out.

"Okay. Fine. I'll climb it," she said. Surely it couldn't be all that different than climbing a tree. Tree climbing didn't scare her, mainly because the trees she climbed weren't terribly tall.

But Evie had never in her life planned to climb a water tower. She had no idea how that was going to go, especially since she was terrified of heights. It was one of the reasons why she hated to fly. Besides, car trips were more fun. You got to see a lot more things.

Thankfully, the first thing she noticed was that there was a ladder attached to the side of the huge metal structure. That didn't make her feel a whole lot better. What she really wanted was some kind of a cable that attached her to the thing.

"Are you sure you want to do this?" Dustin asked.

"Absolutely. I don't wanna be seen as a chicken," she said, her stomach churning.

If her mother ever found out about her doing this, she would kill her. There's a good chance she'd ship her right back to Rhode Island, even if just as punishment. But that didn't stop her.

KATE WALKED DOWNSTAIRS FOR BREAKFAST. Her wonderful day with Cooper fresh in her mind, she couldn't stop smiling. They had spent hours in that water, slipping and sliding down the slippery rock into the beautiful pool below them. And there had been plenty of kissing too. Thus her smile this morning.

When he dropped her off the night before, it was late, the moon bright in the sky. She has peeked in to check on Evie, but she was sound asleep, the covers pulled up around her head as they usually were. She didn't want to disturb her, so she quietly closed the door and went to bed herself. All of the physical activity that day had worn her out, so she was fast asleep before ten o'clock.

She could already smell the blueberry muffins that Mia was apparently cooking in the kitchen. It was amazing how she could tell from the different smells what was being prepared. Sometimes, she would close her eyes and imagine that her mother was down there cooking, and what that would've been like to grow up with her.

"Good morning," Kate said, walking straight to the coffee pot. Mia, wearing her normal apron, pulled a pan of muffins out of the oven and set them on the stove top. "Good morning. How was your adventure yesterday?"

Kate grinned like a Cheshire cat. "It was wonderful."

"Gross. I don't want to know any more," Mia said, laughing as she turned the bacon in the hot frying pan.

"We went to this rock water slide."

"Oh wow. I haven't thought about that place in years. We should take Evie over there one day. I bet she'd love it."

Kate looked around the kitchen. Travis was sitting at the table, drinking a cup of coffee and looking at his phone. She could also see Sylvia and Jack on the back patio, also drinking coffee. They seemed at odds over something, but Kate wasn't going to let anyone's bad time ruin her good mood.

"Where is Evie?"

"Don't know. I assumed she was still upstairs in her bedroom," Mia said, looking around.

"Let me go check. Maybe she's just over sleeping."

Kate trotted back up the stairs, still not overly worried. Evie loved to sleep late, and she was probably just getting in some extra hours before she had to start getting up for school again on Monday.

She opened the door to her daughter's room and her breath caught in her chest. The pillows and covers were still arranged the same way they had been the night before. For a moment, she feared the worst, that her daughter wasn't breathing or something. She ran over to the bed to shake her, quickly realizing that Evie wasn't there at all.

"What in the heck?" she said out loud to herself. She looked up at the window and noticed that it was unlocked.

She ran downstairs, calling out to Mia. "She's not in her room. She wasn't here last night. She put pillows under her covers and her window is unlocked!"

"What? Oh my gosh. She snuck out?"

Travis stood up and walked over to them. "Everybody take a breath. Let's call the police department and see if they know anything."

Just as Kate was pulling out her phone, there was a knock at the door. Her heart was pounding now, and her stomach felt nauseous. Through the window she could see that a uniformed officer was standing outside. Fearing for the worst, she tried to prepare herself as she ran toward the door.

She flung open the door. "Is this about my daughter?"

"Are you Kate Miller?"

"Yes. My daughter is Evie. Is she okay?"

"Yes ma'am. She's fine. She's at the police station."

Kate was completely confused. "At the police station? I don't understand." Mia and Travis walked up behind her, her sister putting a hand on her back to stabilize her.

"Ma'am, were you aware that your daughter was out at a party next to the water tower all night?"

The color felt like it was draining out of her face. "No, I wasn't."

"Did you not check to see if your daughter was in her bed last night?"

"Of course I did. I just realized that she had put pillows under her covers and snuck out the window."

"I see. Well, she's in some big trouble. Along with several others."

"She doesn't even know anyone, well except some boy from high school. She hasn't even started there yet."

"Well, apparently she made a nice big group of friends, and they climbed the water tower last night and defaced it. At this point, she's got two charges of trespassing and criminal mischief against her. There might be more coming."

"Oh my gosh…" Kate said, leaning over and putting her hands on her knees. "I feel like I can't breathe."

"Come over here and sit down. Mia, why don't you get her some water?" Travis helped Kate to a chair and then walked back to the front door. "Sheriff, I'm sure this is just regular teenage mischief. I grew up here, and we always climbed that water tower right before school started. I'm sure you know it's been a long time tradition."

"Well, maybe that's so, but I just took over as Sheriff in this town last year, and I won't have that kind of stuff going on in my jurisdiction."

"It sounds to me like you really want to make an example out of these kids, but is that really what you want the public to know about you? That you're willing to throw the book at a bunch of kids who are just excited about going back to school and are just carrying on the tradition of painting on the water tower?"

"Sir, and I don't know how you're related to this, but this is a crime. Trespassing and defacing city property is not tolerated."

Travis nodded his head. Mia just watched in astonishment as he spoke up to the Sheriff. "Well, I think the bigger question is why hasn't the city taken the initiative to make sure that those kids can't access the water tower? We've been doing this for well over twenty-five years now. A little bit of white paint will fix it right up, and I'm sure the kids would be glad to take care of it. But you're going to try to ruin their futures with charges on their records? Come on now, Sheriff. I don't think that's how you want to make a name for yourself in this little town. After all, we all know each other, and that sure doesn't build community around here."

"What exactly are you getting at?"

"Well, just seems to me that you'll be running for an office that requires the voters' support, am I right?"

"Yes, but I don't see how that's relevant."

"Well maybe you come from a big town or something, but we do things differently around here. We are about family and sticking together. These kids didn't mean any harm, and I'll personally take it upon myself to make sure they climb back up the tower and paint over whatever they've done. But I sure would hope, as a citizen of this town, that you, Mr. Sheriff, would also make sure that the children of this town are safe and kept out of such dangerous situations in the first place."

The Sheriff just stood there, his mouth hanging open slightly, trying not to react. "Ma'am, you can come pick up your daughter in about thirty minutes. This time, I won't pursue charges. But I do expect these kids to buy the paint that's going to be required to fix that. I'll have some of my city workers handle it."

Kate stood up and walked back to the door, reaching out to shake his hand. "Thank you, Sheriff. I appreciate your leniency this time, and I will make sure my daughter never does anything like this again."

The Sheriff nodded his head, glared at Travis for a moment and then turned back to walk to his car.

Mia shut the door and stared at him. "Where did you learn to talk like that?"

"If you're in New York City long enough, you learn to get a back bone. Otherwise, people will run you over up there." Travis said laughing.

"Thank you so much, Travis. I didn't know what to say. I had no idea Evie was doing anything like that."

"Kids do stuff. We all did. Don't be too hard on her. New school and all."

Kate smiled. "I better go get her. Mind if I borrow your car, Mia?"

"Of course. Go on ahead."

As Kate walked to the car, she felt her blood pressure rising already. Evie had made so many bad choices in her young life already, and much of it was because of her need to be liked and accepted. What was she going to do with her daughter?

CHAPTER 8

*M*ia couldn't believe what she had just witnessed. Now, as she and Travis stood in the living room together, she didn't really know what to say. She'd never seen that side of him before, the strong, commanding presence. Of course, the last time they spent any amount of time together, they were both just out of high school, still wet behind the ears, as her mother would say.

"Sorry I just kind of took over there." He shrugged his shoulders and then put his hands in his pockets like he'd done something wrong.

"I liked it," she said, admitting it out loud when she hadn't intended to.

"You did?" A slight smile spread across his face.

"I did. And I hate myself for it," she said, shaking her head as she tried to stifle her own smile.

"I hope Kate doesn't strangle Evie," he said with a laugh.

"Oh, it's very likely that she will. That kid, I just don't know what she's going to do with her."

"Yeah, well we all do things as teenagers that we shouldn't. Do you remember the time that we climbed up that very same water tower?"

She covered the grin on her face. "I certainly remember what happened at the top of the water tower. Our very first kiss."

He chuckled under his breath. "That was an unforgettable moment. I never wanted to come down off the water tower."

"Well, that was a long time ago. A nice memory," she said, feeling a little sad. Those first moments of being a teenager were some of her fondest because they included Travis.

"Yeah, nice memories. Listen, I promised my mom I would come over for a visit, so I guess I better be getting on with the day."

She smiled and nodded. "Of course. Don't let me hold you up. I've got plenty around here to keep me busy."

He turned and started walking toward the front door. "Hey, Mia?"

"Yeah?"

"Do you ever do anything for fun? Like anything that doesn't have to do with the B&B?"

She shrugged her shoulders, laughing sadly. "I guess this place is my life now. Without Momma, I've sort of been like a boat that has come unattached from the dock and is just sort of floating aimlessly out in the water."

He looked kind of sad. "That's no way to live."

"Maybe not, but it's what I've got," she said, crossing her arms as a protective mechanism. It was true that her life was the B&B, but it wasn't by choice. She did want more, like friends, hobbies and a partner, but that hadn't been the hand she was dealt so far. Up until Kate came, she'd been alone again, trying to manage it all by herself. Now that she had some extra time, she had no one to spend it with anyway.

"Care to take another canoe ride when I get back?"

She thought for a long moment. And again, she knew she should say no. "Okay. Before dinner?" Why did she keep telling him yes? Her logical mind was apparently on a vacation.

He smiled and nodded. "It's a date."

He closed the door behind him, before she had a chance to correct him. Was it a date? What in the heck was going on with them?

KATE COULDN'T REMEMBER a time when she was more angry at her daughter. As Evie sat in the car next to her, she said nothing, the blood in her veins feeling like it was actually boiling. Now she totally understood that term.

When she had picked her daughter up at the police station, Evie had tried to plead her case, attempted to tell Kate that she didn't do anything wrong. But Kate wasn't hearing any of it. She told her to be quiet and get in the car, and now they were just riding in silence.

She could see Evie out of the corner of her eye just looking out the window, probably trying to figure out what she was going to say when Kate allowed her to speak again.

Finally, they arrived back at the B&B, and Kate stopped the car. She turned and looked at her daughter, her face still red from the anger.

"What on earth were you thinking, Evie?"

"Mom, I'm trying to tell you that I didn't do anything…"

"Are you kidding me right now?" Kate said, throwing up her hands. "They literally found you on top of the water tower. The fire department had to help you get down because you were too scared!"

"You know I don't like heights!"

"Then why in the world would you agree to climb up on top of the water tower? You had to know it was illegal!"

"I really didn't, Mom. All the kids said they do this every year before school starts. Way back, like decades. Why would I think I'd go to jail for that?"

"You better be really thankful for your aunt's friend, Travis. He's the one who talked the Sheriff out of pressing charges against you."

"I didn't do any of the graffiti. I promise you."

"Right now, I wouldn't believe you if your tongue came notarized!" Kate said, using a phrase she'd heard Mia say. Oh no, she was turning southern.

"So you don't trust me? Even though I didn't do anything wrong?"

Kate stared at her, her eyes squinting like she didn't

understand the language her daughter was speaking. "You did do something wrong. Even if you didn't do the graffiti, you weren't supposed to be up on the water tower. You have to use common sense."

"I'm sorry. I was just trying to make friends, and I didn't want them to think I was some kind of a scaredy-cat."

Kate tried to summon how she would've felt at that age. Would she have climbed the water tower? Mia told her that she had done the same thing in high school. Still, she couldn't show weakness right now. Evie would take full advantage of that.

"And, on top of that, you snuck out. You willingly lied by putting pillows under your covers and then you snuck out the window! Anything could've happened to you!"

"I'm sorry, Mom. I didn't mean to let you down. I knew you probably wouldn't let me go to a party like that, and I wanted to make friends. It's going to be really hard going to a brand new school."

"But you wanted this. You said you wanted to stay here. It's not too late for us to go back to Rhode Island and…"

"No. I don't want to go back there. I just made a mistake, and it won't happen again. I'm looking forward to a fresh start."

"Well, I don't think it's hanging around with those people. Stay away from whoever was at that party last night."

"Mom, it was practically the whole school!"

"When you start school on Monday, you go there,

you come home and do homework, you go to bed and stay in your room. No sneaking out and no social activities for at least a month."

"A month? But what about…"

"Don't try me, Evie," Kate said, holding up her hand. "You're on restriction for one month. We will revisit it after that."

"Fine," she said, crossing her arms.

"Be thankful I didn't say you were on restriction for your entire school year. But I can change my mind if I need to."

"No. I'm sorry. A month is fine. And I won't screw up again."

Kate leaned over and grabbed her daughter, hugging her tightly. "Don't you ever do something like that again. You're all I've got, and I shudder to think what could've happened to you last night. That was so dangerous."

"I know. It was stupid," Evie said, her voice muffled and shaking, pressing against Kate's shoulder.

As they walked into the house, Kate wondered what the next few years of high school were going to hold for her daughter. Would she get her act together and go on to big things in her life, or would she always be chasing trouble to try to fill that spot in her heart that her dad had left?

Mia stood in front of the closet door, this time promising herself that she was going to finish cleaning it out. Most of it was just old files, handmade quilts from her great grandmother and other family mementos that she had seen before. But she was going to get that box in the back, just to see what was inside of it since it was something she hadn't seen when her mother was alive.

Just as she was about to reach for it again, and most probably fall down trying to do it, Kate walked through the office door and fell down into the chair behind her.

"Oh, hey. Where's Evie? You didn't have them put her on a work crew or something, did you?"

Kate sighed and leaned her head back, looking up at the ceiling. "Honestly, I don't know what I'm going to do with that girl. She just doesn't think sometimes."

Mia leaned against the closet door frame, her arms crossed. "I know you're mad at her right now, but honestly what she did is something people have been doing around here for generations. This new Sheriff is just taking everything too far."

"Don't tell her that. She needs to understand that she broke the law, and she did something really dangerous."

Mia smiled. "I know you're really scared right now because it seems like she was in harms way, but nobody has ever fallen off of that water tower. And I don't think she'll do something like that again."

"She better not because I can't take it. The thought of her being out there at night by herself…"

"But she wasn't by herself, Kate. She was with a new group of friends. I mean, doesn't that make you feel good that she's already making friends here?"

"I guess so. But not these friends. I can't believe they talked her into doing something like that."

"Well, if doing that is bad and turned you into some kind of a hoodlum, then I guess I'm a hoodlum. And so is Cooper and so is Travis. We all did it." Mia wasn't about to admit it, but she thought Kate was overreacting a bit. This was the country, and kids did stuff like this all the time. Boredom was a big issue in their neck of the woods. They didn't have shopping malls and skate parks to keep them busy. They had Mother Nature's forest land and the water tower.

Kate glared at her. "Again, you're not to tell that to Evie. She'll use it as an excuse to make bad decisions."

"Didn't you ever do crazy things as a teenager?"

" Not really. One time I tried to sneak out, but then I felt really guilty and went back home."

Mia held up her hand. "Whoa, slow down, you crazy kid!"

Kate laughed. "That's why it's so hard for me to raise Evie. She's nothing like I was at her age."

"Well, we don't all turn out just like our parents, do we?" Mia hoped she would one day get the chance to be the mother that hers had been. Until then, maybe she could just be a fantastic aunt.

"Thankfully, no. I mean, I had a good mother growing up, but I'd never want to be my father."

Mia nodded in understanding. "Listen, I need your extremely long arms and legs to help me with something right now."

Kate stood up. "Okay…"

"There's a box in the closet here that I can't reach.
Would you mind grabbing it for me?"

Kate walked over to the closet and Mia pointed to
the box. "The floral one. Right there in the back
corner."

Of course, Kate grabbed the box easily with one
hand and gave it to Mia.

"What is it?"

"That's the thing. I don't know. I've never seen this
box before which makes me think that my mother was
hiding it from me."

"Well, let's dig in."

They sat down in chairs across from each other
where there was a little table in the middle. She didn't
know why her mother had set up the office like she
was going to have clients in there. But that's exactly
what she did.

"I'm a little scared to open it."

"Do you want me to do it?" Kate asked. Mia nodded.

She watched carefully as Kate opened the box and
looked inside. She pulled out a leather bound notebook
or journal of some kind. As she opened it, at first she
didn't look very surprised. But then her eyes widened
and she closed it quickly.

"What?"

"Are you ready for some information about your
father?" Kate asked.

Butterflies zipped around Mia's stomach. That's
exactly what she had been hoping was inside. Maybe
all those years of mystery would finally be gone. Maybe

she would know at least a little something about her father.

"Yes," she said, reaching out her hand.

Kate gave her the journal. As she opened it up and started to read, she felt so many emotions wash over her.

The first thing she noticed was her mother's handwriting. Although it was obviously from her younger years, it had the same flair she was used to, with the long tail her mother always gave to her L's and S's. She ran her index finger across the words, feeling their indentation on the thick paper, and struggled not to cry.

I'm pregnant again. I can't believe it. The doctor told me it wasn't possible, that my lab work showed a condition that would keep me from having another baby. I'm ecstatic. Thank you, God, for another chance! How will I tell him? I'm in shock.

Mia's eyes started to mist. Kate sat across from her, saying nothing, but silently supporting her.

The next entry was just as short as the first.

I couldn't tell JR. It wasn't fair. He's moved on with his life, and I won't tie him down. I won't be the one who takes his opportunity away. I love him more than my next breath, but maybe that means I have to let him go. Push him away. Tell him I don't love him anymore. He deserves more than this small town, and I'm going to make sure he gets the life he's always dreamed of. God, please help me do the right thing for all of us.

Mia stared at the paper. She didn't understand. Her mother never told her father she was pregnant? And then she pushed him away? How could she do a thing like that? She basically stole her father away from her. All those years, Mia assumed he left when he found out she was pregnant. Now she realized her mother hadn't even told him. She was so angry.

"The rest of this is empty?" she said as she turned to the next pages. Empty, all of them.

"They're empty?" Kate asked, as Mia slid the journal across the table to her. She stood up and started pacing around the room like a caged animal.

"I can't believe this! Read it. You're not going to believe what she did!"

Kate quickly read the pages and then closed the journal, placing it back in the top of the box.

"Wow."

"I know, right? She didn't tell my father I even existed? And then she pushed him away? Why would she do such a thing?"

"I'm so sorry, Mia. I know this must be really hard."

Mia threw up her hands. "I feel like I don't even know her. All those years that I asked about him, and she just wouldn't speak."

"You know, maybe she was embarrassed or felt guilty. She was a wonderful mother in every other way, right?"

Mia walked over to the desk and sat down. She stared at the picture of her mother that she kept on the desk now. She felt very different looking at it, and that made her feel sad.

"She was the best mother anyone could ask for. I just don't understand why she lied to me my entire life.

Or at least wouldn't she tell me anything when she was sick? She could've given me some kind of information."

Kate stood up and walked over to the desk. "I don't have the answers. And there's nothing else in the box but some baby clothes and photo albums of people in the family tree. No more journals."

"So all I know is that my dad's name was JR, or at least his initials. And he never knew about me. I mean maybe she told him later and just didn't write it down?"

Kate shrugged her shoulders. "We may never know."

"Well, I could know if the man who matched me on the website would actually respond. "

Mia felt heartsick. She was angry at her mother now, and she may never meet her father. She just needed some time alone to gather her thoughts.

"Listen, I know we probably need to talk about what happened with Evie some more, but I just want to go down and sit by the water for a while."

Kate nodded. "I understand. Go take some time to get yourself together. I'll hold down the fort here."

Mia smiled and squeezed both of her sister's hands. "Thanks. I'm kind of liking having a sister."

Kate chuckled. "Me too."

Mia made her way down to the dock, bypassing Evie's door which was closed. She was sure her niece was probably inside, licking her wounds.

She walked over and sat down at the end of the dock, her feet dangling. She loved this place. Something about looking out over the still waters and the mountains just brought a certain kind of peace to her soul.

"Oh, sorry, I don't want to interrupt." She looked over her shoulder to see Jack standing there, a fishing pole in his hand. Her mother had always told her to be the best host she could, and she was still planning to do that.

"No, not a problem. Feel free to have a seat. I'm just taking some quiet time."

"You sure?"

"Yes, of course," she said, sending her voice up a couple of octaves to try to cover up the fact that she wanted to burst into tears.

Jack put his tackle box on the dock and took the spot beside her. He pulled out a fishing lure and attached to his hook. Then he flung it out into the water, wound it in a bit and waited.

He was a pretty quiet guy, from what she could tell. Certainly he would give her the peace and quiet she needed right now.

"What's got you feeling so down?"

"Oh nothing. Just feeling a bit blue today."

He laughed under his breath. "Now, I wasn't born yesterday. I can always tell when something's wrong with a woman. Y'all get really quiet when you aren't usually that way."

She nodded her head and smiled. "I guess that's a pretty accurate thing to say."

"Look, I'm a stranger. You'll probably never see me again. What better person to confide in?"

She shrugged her shoulders. "Okay, but you might be sorry you asked."

"I don't think so. So what's going on?"

"Where to begin? When my mother was a teenager, she got pregnant and had a child that I never knew about. Years later, she had me. She would never tell me anything about my father. And, as you know, Kate found me on a DNA site recently. We found journals where my mom talked all about Kate's father. How much she loved him and how their parents pushed them apart. Made her give up her baby. Today, I found a journal where my mom actually talked about being pregnant with me, but there were just two short entries. In one of them, I found out that she never told my father that she was pregnant with me."

Jack sat there quietly for a moment, staring out at his fishing line. "Wow, that's some story. You must be feeling a little angry at your mother right now."

"I am. And that's really hard because I've never been upset with her like this. She was the perfect mother. We were as close as any two people could be, and I just don't understand this. I'm upset for me, but I'm upset for my father also.

"I know I'm just a nobody to you, but there has to be a reason why she did it. It sounds like she was a lovely woman, and maybe she didn't make the right choice, but I think you can be safe in assuming she did it out of love."

Mia shook her head. "Maybe she loved my father more than she loved me in the end because she never told me."

Jack looked at her. "I don't believe that's true at all, Mia. I bet your mother made a decision and then regretted it, and then she spent the rest of her life feeling guilty. Sometimes, we don't know how to undo the messes that we've made."

He reeled his line back in, looked at the empty hook and put another lure on it before tossing it back out again.

"Can I ask you something?"

"Sure," he said.

"You and your wife don't seem very happy to be here together. Is there anything you want to talk about?"

He smiled slightly. "Oh, we're fine. We've been married a very long time. It's just that I don't know why she made me come here. This isn't exactly the type of place we normally vacation, no offense. She's been trying to get me to talk about growing up around here the whole time we've been together, and it's just not something I want to talk about."

"Yeah, but how can you be married to someone and not want to share every part of your history with them?"

He shrugged his shoulders. "Some things are just better left in the past, especially those that cause a lot of pain."

"Well, I know I'm a lot younger than you are, but I'll give you a piece of advice. Never bottle up your emotions away from the people you love. They love you for a reason, and I'm sure that you can trust Sylvia to understand."

"I'll take that under advisement," he said, reeling in his line again. "Boy, the fish aren't biting today."

"Yeah, Travis didn't have much luck the last time he

was out here either. Maybe I need to get somebody to come stock it again."

"I like that Travis. He's a good guy."

She nodded. "Yeah, he is. In fact, we're supposed to go on a little canoe ride here shortly."

Jack stood up. "Well, I don't wanna get in the way of that."

Mia chuckled. "Nothing is going on. We're just very old friends."

"Mia, I was born in the morning, but not this morning," he said, raising his eyebrows. "Well, I'd better get on with the rest of my day. I think Sylvia wants to go shopping this afternoon." He rolled his eyes and sighed.

"Have fun!"

Jack turned one more time. "I hope you find a way to forgive your mother. She seemed like an amazing person from what you've said."

"She was. She *is*," Mia said.

As she watched him walk off, carrying his old, beat up looking tackle box, she wondered what he and Travis had talked about that day they went fishing. She was pretty sure Jack knew a whole lot more than he was letting on.

CHAPTER 9

*M*ia tossed a piece of bread into the water. Her favorite duck, who she had aptly named Donald, swam over, pecked at the water and immediately swallowed the bread. Travis chuckled.

"Do you remember when we used to sit out here for hours feeding the ducks? And there was that mean one, Fred, who used to grab the food right from our hands and then try to peck us in the eye?"

Mia smiled. "I was so happy when that duck finally died."

Travis started laughing. "And do you remember that time we stole the freshly baked poundcake your mother made and came out here and fed it all to the ducks? I thought she was going to kill us!"

"How were we to know it was for the church picnic? She ended up having to take some blueberry muffins we made out of a package right before we left. Sacrilege!"

Mia loved reminiscing with Travis. He was one of

the only people she knew, other than Raven, who had memories with her from that time in her life.

"How's your dad?" Travis looked a little shell-shocked, like he wasn't expecting her to ask the question.

"Hanging in there."

"Has hospice been called in?"

Travis shook his head. "Not yet."

She felt like he was being tightlipped, but she decided not to press further since she knew just how hard it was to have a parent so sick. She felt terrible for him, and wished that there was some thing she could do.

"So, what made you decide to come back out on the lake with me?"

"I don't know. It's nice to reminisce about the good old days, I guess. Remember homecoming in our junior year?"

"How could I forget? You wore the turquoise dress with all the sequins."

She giggled. "I looked like a little mermaid."

"You looked beautiful," he said, looking at her. "I remember thinking I couldn't believe I got to date somebody as pretty as you."

"Well, I remember thinking I couldn't believe I got to date Travis Norton. Every girl in school wanted to go out with you. I never understood why you picked me."

He stared at her, his eyebrows furrowed together. "Are you kidding me? When I met you, it was like meeting this adorable little pixie that I could carry around in my pocket. You always made me smile, and I never had any interest in another girl at our high school."

"I wish things could've…" she started to say, then stopped herself.

"Could've what?"

"Nothing."

There was no use rehashing the past and what could've been. Those days were over, and there was way too much water under the bridge. Plus, he lived in New York, and that much was probably never going to change.

"Listen, Mia, I need to talk to you about something…"

She put up her hand. "Travis, please don't. Let's not ruin a very nice afternoon."

"But you don't understand…"

"There's nothing to understand. There's a lot of water under this bridge, and we've changed a lot since those high school days. Let's just keep the nice memories and try to stay in touch after you leave."

He looked let down, but she wasn't sure why. What did he think was going to happen? Did he think she was going to start dating him again while he lived in New York City?

"Right. I understand." He picked up the oar and started moving toward the shore again. "But, just for kicks and giggles, what do you think would've happened if I never left Carter's Hollow all those years ago?"

She shrugged her shoulders slightly. "Who knows?"

"Just humor me. What do you think wouldn't happened?"

Mia thought for a moment. "I guess I always thought we'd be one of those happily ever after couples who gets married in a big ceremony and then settles down to have an army of kids."

Travis smiled and nodded. "Sounds like a plan."

"Sometimes plans just don't work out," she said, looking back toward the B&B.

As they rowed toward the shore, she found herself lost in thought, visualizing what could have been.

"I'M GOING to be sad to leave here in a couple of days," Sylvia said as she took a bite of her chicken and dumplings. Mia had opted for an easier dinner tonight, just serving that and a side salad. Later, they would have lemon poundcake that she had thawed out from her freezer. It was one that her mother had made months ago before getting too sick to bake.

"Well, I hope you two will come back and visit one day. I know it hasn't been your favorite vacation, Jack," Mia said, with a wink.

"It's growing on me. I can see why you love it here. There's just a certain energy, but I can't put my finger on it."

"That's Momma. She's still in this place, always. In fact, I've been talking with the library about all of the books she left behind, and they're thinking about opening a room dedicated in her name so we can display her collection."

"Really? That's amazing!" Kate said. "Her memory would be honored, and her books would go to good use. I like it!"

"So, how was your first day of school, Evie?" Travis asked.

"Pretty good. I mean, school is school. But I'm finding my way around better than I thought I would."

"And you're not hanging out with the wrong people, are you?" Kate asked, a look of warning on her face.

"No, Mom," Evie groaned as she looked down at her food.

"Good."

"Evie, you don't look so much like your mom. I think you might look a little bit more like your aunt Mia," Jack said with a wink.

"Mia told me that I look like my grandma."

Mia smiled. "She is the spitting image of my mother. Actually, I found a picture of Momma when she was younger in a box the other day. I put it on my desk in the living room to frame. Let me grab it so I can show you, Evie."

Mia walked over to the desk and picked up the picture. She walked back to the breakfast room and handed it to Evie.

"Wow. We do look a lot alike! Even our hair looks the same."

"Mind if I take a look?" Jack asked.

"Now, Jack, that might be too personal," Sylvia said, nervously. Her voice shook as she said it.

Jack looked at her, confused. "A picture is too much?"

"I don't mind at all," Mia said, handing Jack the picture.

What happened next defied explanation. He stared at the photo, Sylvia looking down at her plate like she was about to go before a death panel.

Jack looked at the photo like he was seeing a ghost. He didn't say anything, just gripped it in one hand, his eyes fixed to it.

" Are you okay? You don't recognize my mom do you?"

He cleared his throat. "No. I mean, maybe. She might have grown up near me."

"Oh wow. That would be so great if you had any old stories or…" Kate said.

Jack stopped her. "I don't. I just thought she looked a little familiar, but I might be wrong about that."

Mia felt very uncomfortable now. There was definitely something going on with Jack and his wife, but she couldn't put her finger on it. And now, was there some possibility he actually knew her mother? This whole thing was weird.

"You know, I'm feeling a little sick on my stomach. I think I'm going to go upstairs and lie down," Sylvia said suddenly.

Jack gave her a look. "Yeah, let me come help settle you in. Thanks for dinner, ladies. Sorry we had to cut it short."

Sylvia quickly hurried up the staircase with Jack not far behind.

"What on earth?" Kate said.

Mia stood there, looking at the picture that was still laying on the table where Jack had been sitting. "Something is off. Do you think he knew our mother??"

"It sure seems like he's hiding something," Evie interjected.

"You know, when we were fishing the other day, he talked like he had some history here he wanted to forget. Maybe it's about that?"

"What would Momma have to do with it? I've talked to him about her a couple of times, but he didn't seem to know her."

"Yeah, but is this the first time he'd seen her photo?" Kate asked, her eyebrow raised.

"I assume so. Although he could've looked at her pictures on the mantle any time."

"He never goes in the living room much. He always goes from the upstairs to the kitchen and then to the lake. Maybe he just hadn't seen them." Evie said.

Mia didn't know exactly what was going on, but the next time she saw Jack, she certainly planned to get to the bottom of it. If he knew more about her mother, she wanted to know what it was.

SYLVIA STOOD AT THE WINDOW, staring out over the mountains. Jack was getting really tired of her not turning around and facing him.

"I asked you a question."

"What?"

"Sylvia, why did you really bring me here?"

"I told you. I just wanted you to reconnect with your roots…"

"Dang it! Don't lie to me! Tell me the truth," he said, gritting his teeth.

She slowly turned around, tears running down her face. "I think you already know the truth."

" Are you saying she's my daughter?"

"Yes."

"How did you figure this out?"

"Remember when I told you we were going to do some genetic testing with the doctor and they gave me that kit?"

"Yes."

"Well, that was really for that online DNA site."

Jack ran his fingers through his hair, confusion written all over his face.

"Why would you do that?"

She threw her hands in the air in desperation. "Because you won't open up to me! All these years, I knew you were hiding something, and that it had to do with where you came from. So, I took a chance to see if maybe you had a child out there you didn't tell me about."

"You had no right!"

She stared at him, her hands on her hips. "No right? I've been your wife for twenty years, Jack! How is it that I have no right to know that you had a daughter all this time?"

"I didn't know she existed."

"What?"

"Charlene never told me. She let me go off and start a new job and told me she wasn't in love with me anymore. I didn't know she was pregnant."

"Oh my gosh. So you didn't abandon your daughter?"

"I would think you would know me well enough to know I would never do something like that."

"You have to tell her."

"I think she already knows," he said, running his hands over his face.

"I'm sorry I didn't tell you. When I saw you had a match, and she told me where she lived, I just couldn't help myself. I needed to see her. I wanted to figure out if you had a connection to her."

"This isn't okay. The fact that you did this without consulting me is something we are going to have to work through."

Sylvia nodded. "I understand. I'm sorry. I just thought if I told you, you wouldn't agree to meeting her. And I immediately closed my DNA site account as soon as she messaged you because I felt so guilty."

"It should've been my choice, Sylvia."

"You're right. Are you going to talk to her?"

"Right now, I need to think. I think I'll go take a walk."

As Jack slipped down the stairs and out the front door, he couldn't believe he had a daughter. Never in his wildest dreams did he think Charlene was pregnant, but now he had a piece of her in this world and he didn't know what he was going to do.

~

MIA WALKED around the town square, taking some quiet time before she had to get back home and prepare dinner. She didn't know how that was going to go. Would Sylvia and Jack be sitting at the table, or would they check out early in an effort not to have another awkward meal together?

She was still wracking her brain as she walked, looking at all of the shop windows in her little town. She loved that everything there seemed like time had stood still. They still had a barbershop, a diner and even a soda fountain in the back of the drugstore. Walking down the sidewalks always made her feel calmer, and right now her brain was buzzing in circles.

What was she going to do about Travis? Her feelings for him were bubbling under the surface, just like they had been for all those years, but she knew he'd be leaving at some point. She couldn't go through all of that again.

And then there was Jack. He obviously knew something about her mother and just wasn't saying it. Did he know her history? Did he maybe know who her father was? She hated confrontation, but she needed to talk to him and find out exactly what he knew.

She stopped under her favorite magnolia tree and sat down on the park bench. It was an old one, with black wrought iron and rusty spots around the scrollwork. The wood slats had finally been replaced a few years back, but they were starting to weather now. She remembered sitting with her mother on this same bench a couple of years ago, having an ice cream cone and laughing about this or that.

She missed her so much. And yet she was still angry at her.

They had always promised not to keep secrets, but her mother had kept so many. About Kate. About Kate's father and now about her own father. She just didn't understand.

Mia was an open book, probably giving way too much away to people who didn't deserve it. But it was a part of her nature to want to have deep conversations and connections, and it was something she didn't seem to be able to maintain with a man so far.

She took a sip of her iced coffee, something she reserved as a treat for herself on the bad days, and decided to do a little people watching.

There was Esther Haynes walking down the street with her tiny little dog and her very large rear end. It didn't fit her body, and Mia often wondered if she had it surgically placed there. At any point, she looked like she might topple over backward and bounce right back up again.

And then there was old Mr. Reginald. That man had the worst demeanor of anyone in town, and most people were scared of him. He had a permanent scowl on his face, and he always had a pipe sticking out of his mouth as he waddled down the sidewalk with his baggy pants and red suspenders.

Of course she saw families too, little kids with parents, eager to get to the ice cream shop. When she looked at families, she longed for her own. Oh, how dreams don't always become reality.

But then she saw something she didn't expect. Off in the distance, down in front of the dry cleaners, there was Travis's mother. She was fiddling with something in her purse, and she looked like she was waiting for someone. Assuming it must've been Travis, Mia decided to walk down and say hello. She had always enjoyed spending time with his mother, and they hadn't had a conversation in so many years. Now that Travis was home for a while and they were cordial, maybe she could have a relationship with his mother again.

She started walking that direction, but Travis's mother hadn't seen her yet. Just as she got about fifteen feet away, the person she was waiting for came out of the dry cleaners with a stack of shirts on hangers. It was Travis's father.

She stood there, frozen in place. He didn't look sick. He had plenty of color in his face, and he certainly wasn't gasping for breath or anything. She ducked behind a brick building, around the corner from the drugstore and then popped her head out to watch them. They smiled and talked before walking to their car and driving off.

She leaned against the cold brick and tried to get her heartbeat to slow down. Travis had told her a huge, intricate lie to get her to agree to let him stay at the B&B. But why?

She felt so betrayed. How could he lie about his father being sick? There was only one way to find out, and she was about to do a whole lot of confrontation. This time, she was ready.

TRAVIS WALKED out of the B&B and headed to his car. He had some errands to run today, and he had promised his mother that he would stop by the pharmacy and pick up her prescription that she'd forgotten to get when she was in town.

"Travis Norton?"

He looked up and saw Cooper standing there, trimming some hedges out front.

"Cooper. I would say it's good to see you, but we both know I'd be lying."

Cooper's eyes widened. "Mia did tell you that we made up, right? I mean, I'm kind of dating her sister."

"Yeah, she told me all of that. And I told her what I thought about it."

Cooper put down the trimming shears and walked over to Travis. "Look, man, I know I was kind of a jerk in high school…"

Travis took a couple of steps forward. "Do you know how many times I wanted to kick your butt? When Mia told me some of the things you did to her, I had to restrain myself."

Cooper held up his hands. "That was a long time ago. I was a bully. But, like I said, Mia has forgiven me. I hope you can too."

"Words don't mean anything to me, Cooper."

"Well, if you're around long enough, I'll make sure

that you see action also. I'm a different person, and I'm embarrassed about who I was back then."

Travis stared at him for a moment. "I hope you're right."

"Good to see you, Travis," Cooper said, as he walked back over to the hedges. Travis turned to get into his car and then saw Mia pulling into the driveway at a rapid clip.

"Oh, hey. I was just about to text you and see if you might want some help getting dinner ready later…" he started to say.

She stomped over to him, anger very apparent on her face. He'd seen this side of her before, and it was never good. Tiny as she was, she was a spitfire through and through and he had a good feeling that he was about to get his butt chewed out for something.

"Travis Norton, the nerve of you to lie about your father being so sick! Why would you do that?"

Travis cut his eyes over at Cooper who was obviously listening to their conversation but pretending he wasn't.

"What are you talking about?" he said as quietly as he could, but knowing he should just come clean.

"Don't pretend that you don't know what I'm talking about. I'm not a fool!"

He sighed and looked down. "How did you find out?"

"I saw your mother and father in town. Your dad looks like the picture of health."

Travis leaned his head back and rubbed the palms of his hands over his eyes. "Look, I'm sorry. My dad definitely isn't the picture of health. He has emphysema, but it's under pretty good control. But he does have to wear oxygen at night."

Mia just stood there, glaring at him. "Travis, you know as well as I do that you did not come back here because your dad was on his deathbed. You used that excuse to stay here at the B&B, knowing I would not tell you no, especially having just lost my own mother."

"You're right. I told you that because I knew you'd let me stay here if it had to do with one of my parents."

"But why? Why on earth would you lie about something like that?"

He looked back at Cooper. "Can we talk about this on the dock? There are too many listening ears around here!" he said loudly. Cooper turned his head and went back to trimming.

Mia nodded and followed him down to the dock, her arms crossed the whole time. He could hear her tiny feet slamming into the gravel on the driveway all the way down, definitely trying to make her point of how irritated she was. When they finally stopped on the dock, he was just thankful she hadn't pushed him in yet.

"Mia, when I left here all those years ago, I thought I was doing the right thing. Every time I wanted to write you a letter, I felt like I had to have some level of success to save my pride. And then the years passed, and it became apparent to me that there was no coming back here. I thought you would hate me, and I didn't feel like a success taking pictures of hamburgers and hotdogs. I just kept waiting until I had some level of success so I could come back home and show you this great life. That never happened."

"Travis, what are you getting at? "

"After my wife died, I did a lot of soul-searching. I looked at where I was living, what I was doing, and I decided I just couldn't keep living a lie. I loved my wife, don't get me wrong, but you were always there."

"If I was always there, why didn't you at least send me a Christmas card or even a note when my mother died?"

"Because I felt like it had been too long. I didn't feel like I had an opening to come back into your life."

"So you cooked up this story about your father because you knew that would be your only way to get me to talk to you again?"

He closed his eyes and nodded. "Yes, and I'm really sorry. It was juvenile, and I should've just been honest with you from the beginning."

She turned around and started pacing back-and-forth on the dock and then stopped in front of him again. "I still don't understand what you're trying to say."

"I'm trying to say that I'm back in Carter's Hollow for good. I socked away as much money as I could over the last couple of years to live on, and I'm going to start some kind of business here. Something to do with real photography and not pickles and onions."

She stared at him, her eyes open wide. "You're staying?"

"I came back here because I want to win you back."

She looked like she had seen a ghost. " And what if I don't want you back?"

"Then I guess that's the price I'll have to pay for being a stupid kid all those years ago."

"Travis, I can't promise anything…"

He took a chance and grabbed both of her hands, looking down into her big, doe-like eyes. "I'm not asking for promises. I'm just asking for a chance."

CHAPTER 10

*K*ate stood in the office, her hands on her hips. "He lied? About his father being sick? Who does that?"

"Apparently, Travis does that. I don't know what to think about it."

"Are you considering actually taking him back?"

"I can't even think about any of that. Right now, I need to know what Jack knows about our mother."

"That should make for a great dinner conversation," Kate said with a laugh.

"So, what's up? You said you needed to talk to me about something?"

Kate sat down across from her. "I have an idea. Something I think would be a great opportunity for the business, and a way to also honor our mother."

"What do you have in mind?"

"Honey bees."

"Honey bees?" Mia said, her head cocked to the side.

"I want to start a beekeeping operation so that we

can produce our own raw honey and sell it all over the country. We can have a website, and we're going to call it 'Sweet Charlene's'!"

"You're kidding me, right?"

Kate looked sad. "No, I'm not kidding. I thought you would think this was a great idea. Just think about it. We'll have a great income stream because people love raw honey. It's much healthier, and I think it's like an antibacterial or antiviral or maybe both!"

"I'm in the bed and breakfast business, Kate. I don't know the first thing about raising honey bees. Plus, I'm allergic to bees and terrified of them! Didn't you see me run from one the other day? I almost ran right into the lake!"

"Mia, I'll take care of everything. With just a little bit of funding…"

"Have you looked at our books lately? I'm not even sure how we're going to pay all of our bills this year if we don't get more visitors here, and you're talking about investing in honey bees?"

"I just think it'd be a great side business for us. We could get labels made that say 'Sweet Charlene's Raw Honey'. We might even be able to sell it online around the world."

"Do you really think so? I mean, you can go right down to the grocery store and buy honey."

"This isn't regular honey. That stuff is basically all sugar, made in a factory. This will be home grown and we can advertise Sweet Tea B&B with it. Maybe even sell our own teabags so they can have tea with honey. There's so many different options!" Kate said, standing up and pacing back-and-forth in front of the desk. Mia had never seen her so excited about something.

"I don't know, Kate. That's a lot to think about."

Kate smiled. "But you're not saying no?"

"You're too excited for me to say no right now."

Kate started laughing. "Good. Just give it some thought. I'm not asking you for an absolute yes. I'm just asking you to think about it."

Where had she heard that type of phrase before? Oh yes, with Travis just a little bit earlier. Everybody wanted her to think about things, and her brain was so full she could hardly stand it.

"Fine. I'll think about it. But I'm not making any promises."

Kate ran around the desk and gave her a quick hug. " Okay, but I'll need an answer soon because we'll have to put in our order for the honey bees."

Mia stared at her. "They'll mail you the honey bees?"

Kate nodded her head. "I can't wait! This is going to be so exciting!" she said as she trotted out of the room.

Mia felt like she needed a giant bottle of wine.

JACK STOOD at the edge of the dock, knowing full well that Mia would see him out there soon and probably have some questions. He and Sylvia had skipped dinner, and he was pretty upset with her even now. She was up in the room packing, getting ready for the trip back to Nashville the next day.

Still, he knew he had to do something. He had to come clean with the daughter he never knew he had.

"I figured I would find you here."

He turned around, not shocked at all to see Mia standing there, her hands in the pockets of her white shorts. She was a tiny little thing, not at all like her mother. Charlene had been average height, so he wasn't sure why Mia was so small. Must've been somewhere back in the family generations.

"Sorry we missed dinner. Just trying to get ready for the trip back tomorrow. It's been a pleasure staying here."

Mia got right to the point. "You knew my mother. I *know* you did." She stared at him with an intensity that made him uncomfortable, even though he towered over her quite a bit.

"Mia, I don't know how to say this exactly so I'm just going to be blunt because that's my personality."

"Don't worry. I'm used to it. My sister is the same way."

"I'm your father."

Her face went white, and she put her hand on her chest. For a moment, he worried she might be having a heart attack or something.

"Mia, did you hear me?"

"I heard you," she said softly, still staring at him like she was looking at an alien.

"I think it's important for you to know that I didn't know about you."

"I know. I read that in Momma's journal."

"I also think you should know that I didn't set up

the profile on the DNA site. Sylvia did that without me knowing and then brought me here. I only found out when I saw your mother's picture."

"I think I need to sit down."

Mia walked over and sat on the edge of the dock, her tiny legs dangling over the side. Jack joined her, much like he had the other day when he was fishing.

"I know this is a lot to take in. It has been for me too."

"So, you're JR?"

"Jack Ronald Townsend, in the flesh. I was called JR back in those days."

"Can you tell me what happened? Why didn't my mother want to tell you about me?" She continued staring into the water, like she just couldn't bring herself to look at him.

"I don't totally understand it myself. Your mother and I had known each other all the way through school. Met way back in grade school. She was a beautiful thing with that thick, dark hair and those great big eyes. They look a lot like yours," he said, looking over at her. "We were in love. And I went away for a time, but I came back. I intended for us to get married, start our lives together but then I was offered this great job opportunity. I wanted her to come with me, but she didn't really want to go. She liked it here. You know, this place was in her veins. I was ready to give up the job, but she knew I really couldn't stay with my parents anymore because we had some bad blood. She wanted me to do well, so I guess she lied to me by telling me that she didn't love me anymore. I left town and that was that."

"Kind of like me and Travis," she mumbled under her breath.

"I'm sorry, what?"

"Oh nothing. So, I don't understand something. Why did you go away in the first place? I mean before you came back the last time."

Jack sucked in a deep breath and then blew it out slowly. "There's more that you don't know, Mia. And there's also more that Sylvia doesn't know. I haven't figured out exactly how to break that to her yet."

"What do you mean?"

"Your mother and I were in love from the time we met. We dated in high school, and then something happened. She got pregnant."

"Yeah, with Kate's dad."

Jack looked at her for a long moment. "Mia, I *am* Kate's dad."

Again, Mia put her hand on her chest. "What? How is it possible that we have the same father?"

"Our parents wouldn't let us be together. Charlene got sent off, and I got sent away to a military style camp. So when I came back those years later, it was because I was finally on my own and I wanted to be with her. And we were together for a time until I got that job opportunity."

"So she sacrificed herself to give you your dream job?"

"Something like that. Although if I had known she

was pregnant with you, I would've never left her side. Everything would've been different."

He looked out over the water. The whole time he had been at Sweet Tea B&B, if he was honest with himself, he had felt Charlene's presence there. He couldn't put his finger on what it was until he saw her picture. Once he'd realized he had been staying in the house where she lived up until her dying day, it was almost too much to bear.

"We have to tell Kate."

"We have to tell Kate what?"

Jack turned around to see Kate standing on the other end of the dock.

"Kate, I didn't see you there," Mia said.

"I just walked down here to make sure everything was okay. I saw you two talking. Figured I should probably be involved since it's about my mother too."

Jack and Mia both stood up, like two kids with their hands caught in the cookie jar. Kate looked at them speculatively.

"Is everything alright here?"

Mia looked at Jack and nodded.

"Kate, I don't quite know how to tell you this, but I found out that I'm Mia's father. I never knew about her, and I didn't know my wife had submitted those DNA tests."

"Wow. I mean, that's amazing. I am so happy for you both!"

"Kate, there's more." Mia said.

Kate looked back at Jack. At least he had one daughter who had definitely gotten his height. She was tall and lean, just like he'd always been. And her nose was definitely from his side of the family. "You see, I was in love with Charlene all throughout high school. But then we got separated, and it wasn't until years later that I came back to see her. That's when she apparently got pregnant with Mia."

"Oh, so you might have known my father? I mean if you dated her in high school, surely you knew about…" Kate suddenly stopped herself and stared at him. "Wait. Are you saying…"

"Yes, I'm your father also, Kate."

Kate and Mia just stood there, staring at each other and then back at Jack. He knew they must both have been shellshocked.

"So, we are full-blooded sisters?" Kate said, cutting her eyes at Mia.

"It appears so," Jack said, smiling slightly. "And I have two daughters. Two very beautiful daughters."

"This is unbelievable," Mia said. She and Kate both started laughing simultaneously. It was more of a hysterical laughter followed by what he hoped were happy tears.

"You're our dad!" Kate said. Jack joined in the laughter.

"And you're my daughters!"

The three of them slowly moved together and formed a group hug. It was one of the sweetest moments of Jack's life.

They stepped back so that Jack could look at them again. "I know your mother is looking down on us right now and smiling so big. She did this. I know she did," he said, wiping a stray tear from his eye. "I always wanted kids, and now I have two!"

"So you want to have a relationship with us?" Mia asked, hesitancy in her voice.

"Of course! This is the greatest blessing I've ever had. I want to build a new relationship with each of you, which means I'll be visiting Sweet Tea B&B a lot more in the future!"

"I just have one question," Kate said.

"What's that?" Jack asked.

"Why is Mia so short?"

Mia slapped her on the arm, and they all went back into their group hug. This was definitely the best day of Jack's life.

EPILOGUE

Octber in the mountains was beautiful. Mia had always loved this time of year, and her mother had too. The leaves had changed to a beautiful mixture of orange and yellow. The smell in the air was also another reason why it was her favorite time of the year. It was a smoky smell, but not one of a house burning down. Instead, it reminded her of the years of campfires burning on their property, where they would roast marshmallows and make s'more's.

Today was an unusually warm day in the valley, so she gathered her family together for a cookout on the dock. The water was freezing cold this time of the year. In fact, one year her mother let some men come over and do some thing called the polar plunge. She never understood why anyone would want to jump into water that cold.

As she finished making the last hamburger patty, she looked around at her family. It wasn't what she ever expected it would be, but it was more than she could've ever prayed for.

Kate was standing near the driveway with Cooper, arm in arm, of course. She was finally getting used to seeing them together, able to put those old memories from high school behind her. Cooper had been so good to her family, making every repair around the B&B without ever taking a dime. His guilty conscience meant really good deals for her.

She also saw Evie standing near the water's edge with her new friend, Dustin. Kate had finally eased up on her, and she was thriving at school. Her grades were good, and she had avoided getting into any more trouble. At least so far.

Travis had also become a part of the family again with Mia agreeing to give things another try. They'd been on a few dates, and her heart still fluttered every time she saw him. She didn't know what the future would hold, but she hoped that it would mean never saying goodbye to him again.

Travis had bought a house near town, and she often went over there for movie night or so that he could cook dinner for her. It was good to get away from the B&B from time to time. Having Kate there to help her meant that some of the load had been taken off of her shoulders, and for that she was forever grateful.

Finally, she looked over at Jack and Sylvia. Jack was manning the grill, wearing one of her mother's aprons and a baseball cap. He was so different than the man she had first met. No longer did he seem uptight and grumpy. It turned out he was a lot of fun, and one of the most caring people she'd ever met. She could totally see why her mother had fallen so in love with him. And he was already turning out to be the type of father she'd dreamed of her whole life.

Sylvia had also become part of the family. Mia didn't think of her as a stepmother, necessarily, but more as an extra friend. She had asked a lot of questions about Charlene and seemed genuinely interested in that part of Jack's life. There was no jealousy, only a desire to know more about her husband and what made him tick.

"Medium well okay?" Jack asked Mia.

"Actually, I like mine well done."

He shook his head and laughed. "You didn't get that part from me."

"Definitely not. Momma liked her burgers burned to a crisp."

They had enjoyed so much over the last few weeks getting to know each other. Jack had stayed longer at the B&B after Sylvia went home, and they spent a lot of time together looking through her mother's things.

She was finally able to get the office cleaned out with the help of her father and Kate. There was a lot of crying, and laughing, during that process. But they were finally able to turn the office into something that Kate and Mia could use.

The library had also opened the extra room to house Charlene's book collection. They put a little placard on the door in honor of her, and that made

Mia's heart smile every time she went to check out a book.

"I meant to tell you that I'm going to be ordering the bees in a few weeks," Kate said, clapping as she walked up to the grill.

"I've got a friend who's an expert beekeeper. He said he doesn't mind coming down here to give you a crash course," Jack said.

"I guess it's a good thing to have a dad with connections!" Kate said, smiling.

It had become so natural for them to call him dad. Mia hadn't expected for everything to have been so easy, but she knew her mother had a hand in that. She was looking down from heaven orchestrating everything, and both women were so thankful to have a caring father in their lives. *Finally*.

Travis walked over and put his arms around Mia's shoulders, kissing her on the top of the head. "You should take a picture of those leaves. They're beautiful."

"I've lived here my whole life. You know I have plenty of pictures of leaves," Mia said, laughing.

Cooper walked closer, not wanting to be left out of the conversation. Thankfully, he and Travis had pretty much mended fences, although Travis would occasionally give him grief about his escapades in high school.

As they all stood together, looking out over the lake and watching Jack cook the hamburgers, Mia had never felt more like a true family. She had everyone that she loved in the world standing all around her, and she would never take that for granted again.

"Well, fine, then I'll take a picture," Kate said, pulling her phone from out of her pocket. "Cooper, stand on the dock so I can have a picture of you for my desk."

He walked over to the edge of the dock and posed like he was in a bodybuilding competition. "Like this?" he said, laughing.

She walked closer. "No. Like this." Without warning, she pushed him straight into the water. Everybody gasped. Cooper popped back to the surface.

"What the heck?"

Kate laughed. "Remember that bet when we played air hockey? It was time to pay the piper."

Cooper came flying out of the water, laughing, and chased Kate all over the yard. "You come here, woman!" he yelled, trying to get her wet.

"No…" she yelled as she ran from him, her long legs keeping her just out of his reach.

"Mom?" Evie called from the other side of the yard.

"Hang on, honey! This man won't quit chasing me!"

"Mom…" she called again. Mia heard something different in her voice and turned around.

"Wait… I'm coming…" she said, still running.

"Mom!" Evie finally yelled. Cooper stopped chasing Kate, and she stopped a few feet from her daughter.

"What's wrong?"

Evie's face looked stunned as she handed her phone to Kate.

"What's going on?" Mia asked, walking closer.

"It's Brandon. He wants to see Evie."

In that moment, Mia knew things were about to get

149

really uncomfortable, but she also knew that Evie had a whole new family to protect her from getting her heart broken by her father all over again.

You can find all of Rachel Hanna's books at www. RachelHannaAuthor.com.

Made in the USA
Las Vegas, NV
29 August 2022

54246700R00090